Whatever After

SINK or SWIM

Whatever After

SINK or SWIM

SARAH MLYNOWSKI

Scholastic Inc.

for anabelle,
my littlest princess

✴ chapter one ✴

My Parents Are in the Way

Should I pack a bathing suit?

Yes. I definitely should.

I stuff my bathing suit — it's pale blue with cute white ruffles — into my bright-red suitcase. I'm going to visit my nana in Chicago! I can't wait. My nana is the best. Chicago is the best. And, yeah, I know it's cold to be swimming in Chicago, but my nana lives in an apartment building with an indoor pool and a hot tub.

I'm not really into pools, since I'm not the world's best swimmer.

But hot tubs? I love hot tubs. What's not to love about a big, bubbling bath that melts all your worries away?

Mom and I are flying to Chicago this Friday, only three days from today. It's a long weekend, so I won't miss any school, which is important because I am not a fan of missing school. I am an excellent note-taker and I like hearing everything the teachers say. Also, I don't want to give my new friends the opportunity to forget about me.

So far I have packed:

- the bathing suit
- two bottoms (one pair of jeans, one pair of stretchy black leggings)
- three undies
- three tops (one purple hooded sweatshirt, one white sweater, one light-green shirt with a collar)
- two pairs of pajamas (my orange pair and my navy pair — not my favorites, but they're practically all I have left; I am dangerously low on pajamas.)

The reason I am low on pajamas: When the magic mirror in our basement took my seven-year-old brother, Jonah, and me to

Zamel (where we met Snow White), I accidentally left behind my lime-green pj's. When the magic mirror in our basement then took us to Floom (where we met Cinderella), I accidentally left behind my polka-dot pink-and-purple ones.

Yes, we have a magic mirror in our basement. It came with the house.

I open my jewelry box. My nana bought me a pretty mother-of-pearl necklace for my tenth birthday and I think I should pack it. I don't really understand what the difference between pearl and mother-of-pearl is, to be honest. My nana said mother-of-pearl was more age-appropriate for me. Personally, I think they should call it *kid-of-pearl* if they want it to be more age-appropriate. Anyway, I don't normally wear the necklace to school because I'm afraid it will catch on something and all the mother-of-pearls will go flying across the classroom. But it'll be safe in my suitcase.

My nana bought me my jewelry box, too. The outside features images of all the fairy tale characters. Like Rapunzel with her long hair, the Little Mermaid with her tail, Cinderella in her poofy baker's hat, and Snow White in my lime-green pajamas. Cinderella and Snow White weren't always dressed like that, obviously. Only after Jonah and I changed the endings of their stories. Which was a total accident. We didn't *mean* to change the fairy tales. But everything ended up okay, so no need to worry.

I gently place the mother-of-pearl necklace on top of my navy pj's. I really need to go shopping. But what am I going to tell my parents about my missing pajamas? Maybe that the dryer ate them? It's not like I can tell them *the truth*; Gabrielle, the fairy who lives inside the magic mirror in Snow White's world, told us not to. Maryrose, the fairy who lives inside *our* mirror, has never said a word to us — so who knows what she thinks.

Last Thursday, Jonah and I woke up just before midnight with the full intention of either talking to Maryrose or getting her to take us to another fairy tale.

We got dressed. We snuck down the stairs. We opened the basement door.

And we saw that the lights were on.

My parents were in the basement.

My parents were not supposed to be in the basement at midnight.

Sure, *technically* the basement is their home office. So of course they are *allowed* to work in it. But how were we supposed to get sucked into the magic mirror when our parents were awake and standing right there? We couldn't. It was a problem.

Why were my parents working at the ridiculous hour of midnight? No, they do not work for a twenty-four-hour call center. They do not work for a bakery, either, and they are not getting up to make the doughnuts. Or brownies. (Or crownies. That's an inside joke between us and Cinderella.)

No, my parents started their own law firm when we moved to Smithville a few months ago. And now they're working like crazy people. Jonah and I haven't been able to get to the mirror all week. My parents had a lot more free time when we lived in Chicago.

Now I sit down at my desk and take out my math textbook and notebook. Time for homework. This desk was with me in my old bedroom back in Chicago, but it looks different — bigger — in my new room. I'm still kind of getting used to my new house. I'm not going to lie — it helps that I have a magic mirror.

It also helps that I've made new friends here: Robin and Frankie. Frankie is a girl, although I know it doesn't sound like it. When I have a little girl, I am not going to name her a boy's name. It's too confusing. On the first day of school, Ms. Hellman, the gym teacher, divided up our class into boys and girls and put Frankie with the boys. Frankie's face turned the color of a tomato.

We laugh about it now, though. The three of us: Frankie, Robin, and me, Abby. We're a trio. The terrific trio. Or maybe the tremendous trio. Or . . . I can't think of another word that means awesome that starts with T. There would be a lot more options if we were four or five. Fantastic four. Fabulous four. Famous four. Fun four. But two new friends are good. Two friends are great.

You get what you get and you don't get upset, right? That's what my mother always says. That and: There's nothing to fear but fear itself. And also: You've made your bed, now you have to sleep in it.

For the record, I make my bed every morning. Unlike my brother.

Anyway, I'm going to use all those expressions when I'm a judge. Oh, yeah, I'm going to be a judge when I grow up. Well, first I'm going to be a lawyer, and then I'm going to be a judge, because that's the rule.

I pretend my pencil is a gavel and bang it against my math textbook. "That's my ruling and it's final!" I say out loud. Not bad.

My door swings open and Jonah barges into my room. "What are you doing?"

"Homework," I say.

"Then why are you talking to yourself?"

"Because I feel like it," I snap, embarrassed that he caught me.

He sits on my bed and swings his legs. "Why is your stuff already in your suitcase?"

I turn around to face him. "Why would it not be? Why are you asking me a million questions?"

"I'm bored," he says. "Want to see if we can rock-climb up the side of the house?"

"No, Jonah, I do not. I have to finish my homework, and then I want to finish packing. I'm leaving in three days, you know."

My dad's friend from college and his son are coming to visit this weekend, so my mom and I thought it was the perfect time for some girl bonding. But even if my brother was coming to Chicago, he is the kind of person who would pack the morning of a big trip, not three days before. Actually I take that back. My brother would not pack *at all* because my parents would not trust him to pack. Last time we went away for a weekend, he packed one pair of underwear, two socks, and Kadima paddles. No T-shirts. No jeans. No shoes.

"I don't think you have to pack," Jonah says. "I heard Mom telling Dad that she's exhausted and that her brain is getting fuzzy and that she should probably postpone the trip to Chicago until after the case."

I jump out of my chair. "What? Postpone the trip? *Noooo!*"

He shrugs his thin little shoulders. "Sorry, that's what I heard."

"Are they in the basement?"

Jonah nods.

I run right out of the room and down the two flights of stairs.

Jonah is on my tail. We reach the basement in approximately two seconds flat.

"Mom!" I shout.

I can't help but glance at the mirror. It's still attached to the wall with heavy Frankenstein bolts. Same stone frame engraved with small fairies with wings and wands. Nothing has changed.

Good.

"Yes, honey?" my mom asks, swiveling her chair to face me.

I turn away from the mirror fast before my parents see me staring and realize it's a magic mirror that slurps us up into fairy tales.

No, they probably wouldn't guess all that just by seeing me look at it. Especially since they're so preoccupied with work that they haven't noticed that I'm short two pairs of pajamas, or that their law books are gone from the basement bookcases, or that we're missing one swivel chair. Actually, the swivel chair they noticed, but they just assumed they'd left it in Chicago. The truth is all these things got sucked into the mirror when we visited Snow White.

Anyway. "Mom. Please don't tell me we're canceling the trip to Chicago. Please, please, please don't."

"Oh, honey," my mom says, her forehead wrinkling. "I'm sorry. I was going to talk to you about it tonight, but . . ."

"No buts!" I cry. "It's too late to change your mind. Nana is expecting us! We already have plane tickets! And I already packed!" I stomp my foot on the floor for effect. I know it's babyish, but I can't help myself.

"I spoke to Nana this morning — she understands. She said we should come the next long weekend. And I called the airline and we can switch our tickets, too. Maybe then Dad and Jonah can come with us. We'll stay in a hotel and everything!"

Tears fill my eyes. "I don't want to wait until next time! Next time is months away. And I don't want to stay in a hotel. I want to stay with Nana."

She shakes her head. "I'm sorry, honey. But I'm just too busy. Please try to understand."

I don't want to understand. I cross my arms. I pout. I stomp my foot one more time, just because I feel like it.

I don't want to act like a baby, but . . . but . . . but . . . *Sigh*. I know my mom is *really* busy. And it's my job as the older sibling to act mature. I am ten, after all.

"I *am* sorry," my mom says. "But you know what they say. You get what you get, and you don't —"

"Get upset," I grumble.

Although right now, it's a saying I wish I could *forget*.

✳ chapter two ✳

Grumpy Pants

that night, I toss and turn and turn and toss. I can't sleep.

My still-packed suitcase is sitting on my floor. Seeing it there just makes everything worse, but I don't have the heart to unpack it.

It's 11:45 P.M. and my dad and mom are asleep. They turned in about an hour ago.

Hmm.

I feel a tingle in my belly.

I may not be able to visit my nana, but I can definitely visit fairy land.

I sit up and push my covers off. Yes! I'm going to visit fairy land right now. Why not? I'm wide awake. My parents are not in the basement. Tonight is the night. I know it. I should go!

I look down at the pair of pajamas I'm wearing. Maybe I should change into regular clothes. Although last time, the mirror finally let us in *because* of the pajamas I was wearing. They were the same design as the Floom flag: pink with purple polka dots. But how do I know what clothes will help us get into the mirror if I don't know what story we're going to?

I guess I'll stay in my pajamas. That way if the mirror doesn't let us in, I can at least go straight back to bed.

I spot my open suitcase. Oh! I'll bring my suitcase with me! Why?

1. We are usually in the stories at least a few days. I may as well have a change of clothes with me.
2. It's already packed.
3. Maybe something inside will help us get into the mirror.

So the suitcase is coming, too. I strap on my watch (last time I forgot it and had no idea how much time had passed), then zip my bag and roll it into Jonah's room.

He's fast asleep.

"Hey!" I say, gently shaking him. "Mom and Dad are sleeping. Let's go see the mirror."

He opens his left eye then sits up. "Sure! But why are you bringing your suitcase?"

"To have extra clothes. You can put some of your stuff in it, too."

He climbs out of bed and disappears into his closet. "Like Kadima paddles?" he asks.

My brother is obsessed with playing Kadima. I do not know why. When I'm on the beach, I like to read and relax, not chase a bouncy blue ball with wooden paddles.

"I was thinking more along the lines of clean underwear, jeans, and a T-shirt. You know what, I'll pack for you. You put on your sneakers."

(My sneakers are already on and double-knotted.)

I pack two pairs of his Batman underwear, one pair of jeans, one blue shirt, our toothbrushes, and cinnamon toothpaste. Then I tiptoe down the stairs to the main floor. I lift my suitcase up so that it doesn't bump and wake my parents. It is SO heavy. I motion for Jonah to grab the other end, but he's too focused on his tiptoeing to notice.

I stop at the landing and take a deep breath — there's no sound from our parents' bedroom. We've come so far — we can't get caught now. I open the basement door, turn on the lights, and then we creep down the rest of the way.

In front of us is the antique mirror, twice the size of me. The glass is clear and smooth. My brother and I are in the reflection, of course. We're both wearing pajamas and sneakers. What's worse — we're wearing matching black-and-white pajamas. I hadn't noticed in Jonah's dark bedroom. We look like twins. Like Oompa Loompas. Like Dr. Seuss's Thing One and Thing Two.

"We look like zebras!" Jonah says. His short brown hair is a mess. It's standing up in different directions. I pat down my own curly brown hair. I like to look neat. Also, not identical to Jonah.

I try to look deeper into the mirror to see if I can see Maryrose. She lives inside. At least, we think she lives inside. We don't really know that much about her. Only that she's a fairy and that when we knock three times, she takes us inside different fairy tales. Sometimes. I hope we're wearing — or have with us — the right thing.

"I'll do the knocking," Jonah says. "Ready?"

This better work. It will be pretty annoying if I have to drag this suitcase all the way back upstairs tonight.

"One —"

"Wait! Jonah?"

His hand freezes in midair. "Yeah?"

"Let's try not to mess up the story again, 'kay? We just want to visit and see what's happening. We don't want to change anything."

"Uh-huh," he says. "One —"

"Don't 'uh-huh' me," I state. "I do not want you touching ANYTHING or talking to ANYONE. Not without my permission. Got it?"

"Yes, Mom."

I wag my finger. "No messing the story up. That's a rule."

He twists his bottom lip. "What story do you think it'll be?"

"Hmm. I don't know."

"I like *Jack and the Beanstalk*." His eyes widen. "How cool would it be to meet a giant?"

I nod. As long as he doesn't step on us.

"Or Aladdin! Then we could fly on a magic carpet."

Flying on a magic carpet sounds a little scary. What if I fall off? On the other hand, then I wouldn't need airplanes. "I could take the magic carpet to visit Nana!"

Jonah grunts. "So I can't talk to anyone or touch anything, but you can steal the magic carpet and take it to Chicago?"

"I was kidding," I say. Kind of.

He shifts from foot to foot. "Can we go now?"

"Yes. Just remember: No touching."

"Unless it's stealing a magic carpet."

"Right." Then I shake my head. "No. No touching. No stealing. No anything."

He laughs. "Okay, okay. Can I do my three knocks now?"

"Go."

He does. Almost immediately, there's a hissing sound. The mirror starts swirling and casts a purple light over the room. A second later, it's pulling us toward it like it's a vacuum cleaner.

"It's working!" Jonah exclaims.

"Then let's go!" I grip Jonah's arm with one hand, my suitcase with the other, and step inside.

✳ chapter three ✳

Splash

the second I go through the mirror, I inhale a mouthful of water.

What is happening? Am I in my bathtub? Why can't I breathe?

Everything is blurry, and my eyes sting, so I close them. The water is salty. Bathtub water isn't salty. Also, I'm horizontal, on my stomach, and my elbows are rubbing against the ground.

A sandy ground.

Need air! Can't breathe! Lungs exploding!

I open my eyes, look for the light, and push my face toward it.

And then . . . *cough, cough, cough!* Ahhhhhhhh.

Air. I'm breathing air. Gulps and gulps of air. Who knew air could taste so good? Who needs ice cream when air is so incredibly delicious?

Once I've finished gorging on the air — it's an all-I-can-eat air buffet! — I realize I'm looking at a sandy beach. But I'm not on the beach. I'm in the water, looking at the beach. It's bright out here, too — around noon. What is going on? I twist around and see that a huge wave is about to smash into me. "No!" I yell, and try, unsuccessfully, to get out of its way.

CRASH.

No, no, no, I will not drown! *Cough, cough, cough!*

My heart is thumping, and I push myself to my feet before I can get attacked again. What in the world is happening?

I turn back to face the beach. It's empty. No tourists, no sand castles, no bright-colored beach towels. Just pure-white sand sparkling in the midday sun. Beyond the beach are trees and beyond the trees are mountains. When I turn the other way, there's blue ocean as far as the eye can see. Even as far as my *stinging* eyes can see. Wait a sec. One thing my eyes can't see is my brother.

"Jonah! Jonah, where are you?" Where is he? My heart sinks to the ocean floor.

Just as I'm about to panic for real, he bursts out of the water and gives me a thumbs-up. "How cool is this?" he cries, sopping wet and grinning.

He's here! He's okay! Hurray! "Jonah, get over here now!"

"I'm fine!" he yells back.

Unlike me, my brother loves to swim.

According to my parents, when I was a kid, not only did I refuse to swim in the ocean, but I would cry hysterically when anyone else tried to. My parents. My brother. Strangers. Obviously I'm over that *now*.

Kind of.

CRASH.

Another wave sends me toppling back under the water.

AHHHHHHHH!

Cough, cough, cough!

Okay, fine, I'll admit it: I AM AFRAID OF WATER.

Not hot tubs or baths, but oceans, lakes, and rivers. Also moats, when I happen to come across them. Basically, I am afraid of bodies of water that have animals in them.

I am also afraid of pools.

They seem shallow but then BOOM the bottom's gone, and you're gulping chlorine.

Right now, I need to get out of the ocean, pronto, before it sucks me under for good. As I stand, my pajamas feel like they weigh two-hundred pounds. My sneakers are no longer sneakers. They are now bricks attached to my feet.

"I wonder where we are," Jonah says, swimming up behind me. "Do you think we're in *Jack and the Beanstalk*?"

Oh! Right! We're in a fairy tale! There must be a fairy tale reason for the water, then. My shoulders relax. "Do you *see* Jack or a beanstalk?" I ask. There's no ocean in *Jack and the Beanstalk*.

He scrunches up his nose. Hmm, his nose is looking a little red. He might need sunscreen. Crumbs, I don't think I packed any.

Speaking of stuff I packed — where's my suitcase?

I spin around and around until I spot it a few feet away, floating in the other direction. "Our stuff! We have to get it!"

"I'll get it," my brother says, diving after it. Except the waves are quick and I can see my red suitcase drifting away faster than Jonah can swim.

"Forget it, Jonah!" I don't want him swimming so far out. It's too dangerous.

"But I don't want to lose my Kadima paddles!" he calls.

"You didn't pack them!" I yell back.

"I did when you weren't looking!"

Now I know why my suitcase was so heavy.

Eventually, when the suitcase is nothing more than a red dot in the distance, Jonah gives up and swims back.

Great. Just great. I have nothing to wear but soggy pajamas and hundred-pound shoes. With a large sigh and a lot of effort, I heave myself onto the dry sand.

SQUISH. When I pull off one of my sneakers, a piece of seaweed and a gallon of sandy water spill out.

Jonah is right behind me. "Abby! I see someone! Is that Jack?" He points to the ocean. In the distance, there's a blob moving toward us.

I squint toward the water. I see a head! A guy's head! But it can't be Jack. Jack climbs; he doesn't swim. Also, Jack is about my age, and this guy looks like a teenager. Wait! Behind the guy's head another head keeps bobbing in and out of the water. A girl's head. At least I think it's a girl's head. I can see long blond hair. They're getting closer . . . and closer . . . and . . . Yup, it's a girl. And then behind her is something green and orange. A towel? A floatie?

It's shiny and triangle-shaped and reminds me of a paper fan I had as a kid.

Oh! It's a tail! The girl has a tail!

Which can only mean one thing.

"She's a mermaid!" I exclaim. "We're in *The Little Mermaid*!"

"But who's the mermaid holding?" my brother asks. "Maybe it's Jack?"

"I am one hundred percent sure it is *not* Jack," I snap.

The guy has dark-brown hair and his eyes are closed. His head is rolling from side to side. That's not a good sign.

I can't tell if this mermaid is *the* Little Mermaid or just *a* mermaid. I need to remember the original story. My nana read it to me a million times. I just have to focus, and it'll all come back to me. Too bad there's no *time* to focus.

From about twenty feet away, the mermaid's head bobs above the surf. She looks right at us, gasps, and disappears under the water. A second later, she pushes the guy toward us and swims in the other direction.

"We scared her," Jonah says.

"Wait!" I call to the mermaid. "Don't leave!"

"I thought we weren't supposed to talk to the people in the story!" Jonah exclaims.

Right. Crumbs.

No time to worry about that now.

The guy is sinking under the surface and it's up to us to save him.

* chapter four *

The Real Story

We jump back into the water and each grab one of the guy's arms. He's wearing a yellow shirt and dark-brown pants that are soaked and torn. He's handsome. Really handsome. Floppy brown hair, chiseled cheekbones. Full lips that are tinged blue.

Uh-oh, that's not a good sign.

"Don't drop him!" I order.

Jonah's eyes are wide with worry. "Is he okay?"

A wave crashes into my back and I ignore the question. "Let's just get him to the shore!"

We pull and we heave, and a few minutes later we lay him

down on the sand. I cup my ear against his mouth. He's breathing! "He's okay! Just unconscious, maybe?"

Jonah exhales in relief. "Who do you think he is?"

As I collapse on the hot sand beside him, the original story floats back to me. Prince . . . shipwreck . . . the Little Mermaid saved the prince . . . "Oh! That *was* the Little Mermaid! And this is the prince she saved from the shipwreck!"

"But why was the prince in the water?"

"Don't you remember?" I ask. Nana read him the same stories she read to me. Although I paid attention 110 percent of the time and he paid attention about 10 percent of the time.

He shrugs. "Just start at the beginning."

"Fine," I say. I lie down on the sand and close my eyes, suddenly exhausted. "There was a mermaid. And she was, um, little."

"What was her name?" Jonah asks.

Hmm. Good question. "I don't think she has a name in the actual story."

"Who wrote the story? Was it the Grimm brothers again?"

"No, it was a Danish guy. Hans Christian Andersen."

"He liked Danish? The cheese kind?"

I open my eyes just long enough to roll them at my brother and then close them again. "No, he was from Denmark. The country."

"But the Little Mermaid lived in the ocean, right?"

"Obviously."

"Why are you being mean?" he whines.

"Because you're asking dumb questions!"

"I'm sorry. I'll stop talking. Just go on with the story."

"The Little Mermaid really wanted to swim to the surface but she wasn't allowed until her fifteenth birthday. She had a bunch of older sisters and they'd already done it. When the Little Mermaid was finally allowed to peek out above the water, she saw a prince fall off a boat. Instead of letting him drown, she brought him to shore and saved him."

"That's what we just saw!" he exclaims.

"Exactly."

Beside us, the prince coughs up some seawater. Both of us spring up, but the prince's eyes stay closed.

"So what happens next?" Jonah asks.

"Well, after she saved him, she fell in love with him."

"And then they got married?"

"No," I say. "It's kind of a long story, actually, but what happened is that she hid. She didn't want the prince to see her since she was a mermaid. So when he woke up, he didn't know she had saved him. She went back underwater and asked around and discovered that the only way to get a human on land to fall in love with her was to have two legs. And the only way for her to get two legs was to make a deal with the sea witch. So she went to the sea witch and —"

The prince lets out a loud snore.

"And," I continue, "the sea witch offered to give her legs, but the witch wanted payment. So the Little Mermaid gave her —" I stop. This part is gross.

"Her allowance?"

I squirm. "No."

"Her sneakers?"

"What sneakers? She had a tail."

"Oh. Right. Then what?"

"Her tongue."

"Are you kidding me?" he gasps. "The Little Mermaid gave away her tongue?"

I nod, trying not to picture it.

Jonah's eyes light up. "That's disgusting! Awesome!"

My brother tends to like the gross parts of these stories. He has a stronger stomach than I do. He loves roller coasters. Especially the ones that go upside-down. Not me, thank you very much. I prefer staying upright.

"Well," I say, "technically, it was the Little Mermaid's voice that the sea witch wanted. The Little Mermaid had an amazing singing voice. But she gave that up for legs. Forever."

Jonah shakes his head. "I can't imagine never speaking again."

"Me neither," I say. I doubt you can be a judge if you can't speak. How would you sentence people? "Also, the sea witch added an extra curse to the spell — if the prince married any-one else, the morning after the wedding, the Little Mermaid would . . . would . . ."

"Would what?" Jonah asks. "Have to give the sea witch her fingers? Her nose?"

"*Snoooort!*" groans the prince, but his eyes stay closed.

"Worse than that," I say gravely. "If the prince married any-one else, the morning after the wedding, the Little Mermaid would die."

Jonah pales. "But we don't have to worry, right? Because there must have been a happy ending. The prince fell in love with

27

the Little Mermaid, they got married, and they lived happily after?"

"Well . . ." I hesitate.

Just then we see a splash in the distance. It's the mermaid again. The *Little* Mermaid. Her blond hair, her green bikini top, and her green-and-orange tail peek out of the water and then disappear.

"I see her," Jonah whispers. "Should we hide? Maybe if we run away she'll forget she saw us and the story can continue the way it's supposed to?"

"Yeah," I say, remembering what I'd said back in the basement. That we should stay out of the way so that whatever fairy tale we landed in wouldn't get messed up.

Except maybe I want to mess this one up.

I look at the Little Mermaid and then back at the prince. "Here's the thing. The ending of the real story of the Little Mermaid isn't good. It isn't like the happy ending in *Cinderella* or *Snow White*. In the end of the Little Mermaid's real story, the Little Mermaid *doesn't* get the prince. She doesn't get her happy ending at all. In the end of the real story the prince marries someone else, another princess, and the Little Mermaid . . ." I take a deep breath. "The Little Mermaid dies."

"You're wrong," Jonah tells me. "I saw the movie. The Little Mermaid doesn't die!"

"The movie isn't the real story," I say. "Haven't you ever heard of a Hollywood ending? When the movie writers give the story a happy ending even though that's not what happens?"

"But she can't die," Jonah cries, and bangs his fist against the sand. "That's the worst ending I ever heard!"

I nod. "It definitely is a bummer."

Okay. I think I *do* want to mess up the ending. "I have a new plan. I think we should change the rest of the story."

He twists his lower lip. "I thought that was against the rules."

I throw my hands up in the air. "Maryrose has never even spoken to us! Whose rules?"

He cocks his head to the side. "Your rules."

Oh. Right. "Yes, well, technically changing the ending is against my rules. But maybe that rule is a mistake. I don't want the Little Mermaid to die. I want to give her a new ending — a happy ending."

✳ chapter five ✳

That's What Happened

There's another groan beside me. This time the prince's eyes flutter.

"I think he's waking up," my brother says.

The prince's eyes open all the way. He looks at Jonah and then at me. "Where am I?" he asks, his voice gruff.

"You're on a beach," Jonah says.

"How did I get here? I was on a ship." The prince sits up slowly and rubs his forehead. "I don't remember what happened. Wait. I do remember. There was a storm. I fell overboard. How did I survive?" He notices our soaking wet clothes. "Did you two save me?"

I crouch beside him. "It wasn't us. It was the Little Mermaid!"

His eyes crinkle. "The what?"

"The Little Mermaid!" I point to the water. "She was right there a few minutes ago."

He twists to look but the water is smooth. "What's a mermaid?"

"You know," Jonah says. "Half fish, half person?"

The prince shakes his floppy hair, and I wonder if he lost his crown in the ocean.

"There's no such thing as a half person, half fish," he says. "That's ridiculous."

"It isn't," I say. At home, I'd have to agree with him. If one of my new friends told me that she'd seen a mermaid at the beach I would have to ask her if she'd hit her head recently. But we aren't in Smithville. "Where I live, you'd be right," I say.

"You don't know that," Jonah tells me. "We might have mermaids at home."

"We do not," I say.

Jonah shrugs. "You don't know for sure. He thinks there are no mermaids here, and he's wrong."

Fair point, I guess. I motion around me. "Where are we, anyway?" I ask. From the beach, I spot a path that leads toward a big stone building in the distance. Just as I'm trying to figure out what it is, a bell rings from it. A school?

The prince stretches his arms up above his head. "The kingdom of Mustard."

Jonah and I both laugh. "Seriously?" I ask.

The prince squints into the sun. "Why would I joke about the name of my kingdom?"

"Your kingdom is named after something you put on a sandwich?" Jonah asks.

"Maybe they don't have mustard here," I tell Jonah. "Like how in Floom they didn't have brownies."

The prince shakes his head. "We eat mustard. It's our favorite condiment. We eat brownies, too. We even dip them in mustard."

"That's disgusting," I say.

Even Jonah agrees. "Yuck," he says. "I wish we were in the kingdom of Ketchup."

My brother is obsessed with ketchup. He puts it on everything. Fries. Mac and cheese. Plain bread.

Seriously, plain bread. Now, that's disgusting.

"Brownies in ketchup," Jonah says. "That I'd try."

Now, that's *really* disgusting.

The prince wobbles to his feet. "Who are you?" He eyes our outfits. "You didn't escape from a prison, did you?"

I look down at our matching pj's. Our matching black-and-white-striped pj's. We do look like inmates.

"No," I say quickly. "We're just in our pajamas."

"So if you two didn't save me, how did I survive? Maybe a fisherman brought me in? Or I washed up on a piece of driftwood? Or are you two just being modest?"

"No," I say. "I can barely swim. It was the Little Mermaid — we just dragged you in."

"Aha! So you DID save me! Then I, Prince Mortimer, am in your debt. Would you please accompany me back to the palace so you can be celebrated?"

"But Prince Morty . . . can I call you Prince Morty?" Jonah asks hopefully.

"Only my parents call me Morty."

Jonah pouts, then continues, "But Prince Mortimer, it really wasn't us who saved you."

Hold on. I elbow Jonah in the side.

"Ouch!"

"I just need a minute to talk to my brother," I say, and yank him a few feet away. "We may as well go to his palace," I whisper.

"We might not be able to find the Little Mermaid tonight, and we're going to need somewhere to sleep."

Jonah shrugs. "I'm game if you are. But we're definitely going to mess this story up."

I look out at the water. "Let's hope so."

✳ chapter six ✳

Celebration Time

We're walking up the path toward the building when we run smack into three teenage girls. They all start shrieking the second they see us.

At first I think they're making fun of our matching prison pajamas, but then I realize they're shrieking at the sight of the prince.

"Oh! My! Goodness!" swoons one.

"It's him! It's him! It's him!" cries another, looking like she might faint.

Jonah and I aren't the only ones dressed in matching outfits — the girls are all wearing white collared shirts, yellow skirts, white kneesocks, and yellow patent-leather shoes. A uniform? I guess the building is a school after all.

"Prince Mortimer!" the third girl cries out. "Everyone is looking for you! I'm, like, so happy that you're okay!" The girl has a mouth full of bubble gum and super-curly brown hair. Each curl looks like a Slinky.

I wish my curls did that. I also wouldn't mind a piece of gum. Especially since my toothbrush drowned with the rest of my suitcase.

"I'm fine," the prince says. "But I need to get back to the palace."

"Let me get help!" the girl with curly hair says, and then runs back up the path. The rest of the girls just continue to stare.

A few minutes later, she's back with a bunch of important looking grown-ups, and soon we're on our way to Prince Mortimer's palace.

The hour-long carriage ride swerves us around the beautiful coast. All along the beach are small villas with big outdoor decks and docks and boats. The waves crash against the white sand. The water sparkles like emeralds. The sky is bright blue. Leafy green trees sway in the distance. It kind of looks like the pictures my parents took of their tenth anniversary trip to St. Thomas, which is an island in the Caribbean. Even though Nana came to stay with me and Jonah, we were NOT pleased about being left behind. Jonah was bummed to miss out on the Waterinn Resort's many activities — snorkeling! swimming! kayaking! — while I was bummed that we missed out on the hot tub. Also, I love tall frosty drinks that come with tiny umbrellas, and I'm pretty sure that's what all the drinks are like in the Caribbean.

When we arrive at the palace, there is a crowd of people waiting for us out front. At the center are the queen and king. They're both wearing gold crowns, but they're not dressed like a typical queen and king. Instead of robes, the king is wearing yellow shorts and a yellow-and-white flowered shirt. The queen is wearing a yellow tank dress with a gold belt, gold flip-flops, and big gold sunglasses.

These people really like yellow. Oh — it's probably their official color, since it's the kingdom of Mustard!

Both the king and queen have sun-bleached hair and leathery-looking skin from too many hours spent on the beach. Which is the kind of skin I don't want to have when I'm older. Which is why I always wear sunscreen.

Except for now. Because I didn't realize I'd be going to a beach.

After grabbing the prince in a bear hug, the king turns to us. "Dudes! We are so grateful that you saved our son," he says.

Dudes? I'm not a dude. "It wasn't just us," I say. "A mermaid brought him to shore."

The king laughs. "Sure, dude. Whatever you say. We're just grateful that he's okay. After he disappeared off the ship we assumed the worst."

"You'll be our guest for a few days, won't you, darlings?" the queen asks, not letting go of her son's hand.

"Sure!" Jonah exclaims, gesturing toward the tennis courts to the left of the palace and the volleyball court to the right. "It's awesome here."

He's not wrong.

The palace is amazing. All windows and marble. Yellowish marble. These people take the name of their kingdom seriously.

"Darlings, would you like something to drink?" the queen asks. "Maybe a banana smoothie?"

We nod. That definitely sounds tall and frosty. A minute later a tall, icy yellow drink — with a teeny, tiny yellow umbrella — is plunked into my hand. Hurray!

I slurp it down in twenty seconds. Yum.

Jonah nudges me. "Not bad, eh, darling?"

I laugh. "Pretty good, dude, pretty good."

A maid named Vivian leads us inside the palace. She's about my mom's age, and her brown hair is tied back in a tight bun. She's wearing a perfectly pressed yellow uniform.

Inside the palace, there are yellow flowers everywhere. The rooms are decked out with gold chandeliers and ginormous paintings. Paintings of the ocean, of the king and queen, of the prince, and of other people in crowns.

Vivian leads us upstairs. She opens the door to my room. And by *room*, I mean *suite*. Huge, gorgeous suite.

It's the size of the entire top floor of my house in Smithville. In the middle is a king-sized yellow canopy bed. The room even has a balcony that overlooks the water. From the window I can also see a pool. And a mini-golf course. And a baseball diamond. And a hot tub.

Yes. A hot tub.

Forget the Waterinn — this might be the best hotel ever. Except it's not a hotel. It's Prince Mortimer's house. Our house for the next few days.

Jonah's room is right next door. There's a door between our rooms that connects us if we want to be connected.

"You can unpack here," Vivian says, motioning to a chest of drawers.

"Thanks," I say. "But we lost our luggage. I don't have anything to unpack."

Speaking of stuff in my suitcase, now that I think about it, I bet the reason Maryrose let us in the mirror right away was *because* I had packed a bathing suit. It's a must-have piece of clothing for this fairy tale. She must not be very happy that I let my suitcase vanish in the ocean.

"Nothing to unpack?" Vivian echoes. "I'll ring for the royal tailor at once! You absolutely need something for the prince's welcome-home party tonight!"

I can't help but think about that fairy tale, *The Emperor's New Clothes*. Wasn't there a fake tailor who pretended to sew all these new outfits for the emperor, but the emperor was really walking around naked? Hopefully this tailor will make me *actual* clothes.

A few minutes later, the royal tailor knocks on my door to take my measurements. Then he takes Jonah's and hurries away to get to work.

"In the meantime, get in the hot tub and relax," Vivian orders. "I'll bring you an extra swimsuit."

Okay. If she insists.

I slip on the suit — it's yellow with gold, red, and green polka dots — and make my way outside in a plush yellow robe and matching slippers.

The hot tub overlooks the ocean. I dip my big toe in first. *Ahhh*. Hot and delicious.

As I sink under the steaming water, I think, *I could get used to this*.

After Jonah — in new yellow swim trunks — joins me for a bit, we both return to our rooms to get ready.

My closet is now filled with outfits. Real ones — nothing invisible here. There's a beautiful long, flowy yellow dress with a beaded top and a silky skirt. There's also a simpler cotton yellow sundress. Two yellow nighties. A few pairs of yellow undies. I'm going to look very sunny. Good thing they also gave me a new pair of red sunglasses.

I put on the fancy dress and step out onto my balcony, calling to Jonah to meet me outside.

Jonah steps onto his balcony, which is connected to mine with a short divider between them. He's wearing new yellow pants, a striped yellow-and-white collared shirt, and a massive smile. "I love it here," he says. "This is the best vacation ever!"

"It's not a vacation," I remind him. But honestly — it does kind of feel like a vacation. The view from here is incredible — blue, blue water that goes on forever. Even though it's warm and sunny, the ocean breeze is gentle and amazing. But still. "We have a job to do. We *really* have to find the Little Mermaid before it's too late." I look out into the water, hoping for a glimpse of her. Is she swimming up the coast looking for the prince right now? Where is she?

Jonah pumps his fist in the air. "We have to stop her from dying!"

"So, here's the plan," I say, rubbing my hands together. "We're going to nip this problem in the bud. We're going to stop the Little Mermaid from making the deal with the sea witch in the first place. If she stays a mermaid, then she won't die, even if the prince marries someone else."

Jonah cocks his head to the side. "That's not what I think we should do. I think we should let her make the deal with the sea witch and then help her get the prince to fall in love with her so she can live happily ever after."

What? He can't be serious. "Jonah," I say, "that is the worst plan ever."

He motions around him. "But it's so nice here! I bet the Little Mermaid would really like it."

I wag my finger in his face. "That is a bad plan for many reasons. First of all, it's very risky. If the Little Mermaid visits the sea witch, then she *has* to get the prince to marry her, or bye-bye mermaid."

"Everything has risks," Jonah says. "We keep going through the mirror even though we never know where we're going to end up or if we can get home. Living on land with the prince is the Little Mermaid's dream. We can't tell her not to dream. Everyone has to dream big, right?"

"Of course we have to dream," I say, annoyed. "But if you know your dream is impossible, then you give it up. You find a new dream and you make it work. You get used to it."

He frowns. "That's so sad."

My brother's just not getting it. "Jonah, we didn't want to move to Smithville, did we?"

He shakes his head. "*You* didn't want to move to Smithville."

"Fine, *I* didn't want to move to Smithville. But we did, and now we're okay. We have friends. We have a magic mirror. It's not so bad. You have to learn to make the best of what you have. You get what you get and you don't get —"

He smirks. "Wet!"

"Upset," I say. "Hmm. Maybe that's the whole point of the original *Little Mermaid* story. That she should have been happy with being a mermaid. The Little Mermaid gave up her whole life — her family, her home, her tail, and even her voice — for a guy who didn't appreciate her."

Jonah nods. "That's true. She even gave up her tongue."

"Exactly. If she'd learned to be happy with what she had, she would have been much better off." I squeeze the railing. "We have to stop the Little Mermaid from making the biggest mistake of her life."

He nods. "You're right."

Of course I'm right. I'm always right. Well, not always, but usually. "Now the only issue is — how do we find her?"

"Maybe she'll be at the party?" he asks.

"I doubt she'll be hopping around on her tail," I say. "But maybe someone at the party will know how to find her. Before she makes the deal with the sea witch."

If she hasn't made the deal already.

chapter seven

Party Hearty

As we hurry down the marble stairs, I glance at my watch, which says it's twelve fifteen at night. Huh? It doesn't feel like it's twelve fifteen. Oh, right, that's the time it is back home.

I look for a clock and see that it's six P.M. here. I guess every hour at home is a day here. We have to be back home by seven A.M., the time Mom and Dad wake us up. So we have six-and-three-quarter hours. Which means six-and-three-quarter days here. That's tons of time to find the Little Mermaid a new happy ending and find our portal home.

As long as my watch is right. We did take a bit of a swim — I hope this watch is waterproof.

We hear the music from the ballroom and discover that the event is already in full swing. Since we're both starving, we make a beeline for the buffet. Vivian introduces us to Carolyn, the chef, who's setting up the plates of lobster sandwiches, mac and cheese, corn, and, of course, mustard. Lots and lots of mini bowls of mustard.

Carolyn is wearing a poofy yellow chef's hat and a yellow apron. She's about my nana's age.

"Have you guys even tried ketchup?" Jonah asks Carolyn. "I think you'd like it."

She makes a sour face. "Ketchup? Too tomato-y."

Jonah sighs.

As we munch on the delicious food, we chat with the guests. Everyone wants to meet us, the children who saved the prince.

"It wasn't just us!" I tell anyone who will listen. "A mermaid was the one to actually save him — we only helped with the last step."

"A mermaid! What's that, darlings?" asks the queen.

"A half fish, half human," I explain.

"That's impossible," the queen laughs. "You two darlings have fantastic imaginations!"

"Have you ever heard of mermaids?" we ask Vivian as she folds yellow napkins. "Half fish, half human?"

"No such thing," she snaps.

How are we going to get someone to tell us how to find the Little Mermaid if no one has ever heard of mermaids?

"Psst! Hey!"

Jonah and I turn around to see Carolyn the chef beckoning from a long hallway.

"Does she mean us?" I ask.

"I guess so," Jonah says. "Let's go!"

Before I can respond, Jonah has already taken off after her. And of course, I follow. I can't let him chase kind-of strangers by himself.

"I heard your questions and I have something to show you," Carolyn whispers.

"About mermaids?" I ask.

"Shhhh!" She opens a door that leads to a winding staircase. "Follow me."

We take the stairs down a floor until we're in the basement, and then we follow her into a small room.

"You should see this." In the center of the room is a small bed covered with a yellow comforter. To the left is a dresser. She opens the bottom drawer and takes out a drawing that's about the size of my hand.

"Look," she says. "Careful."

I take the drawing and realize that it's of a woman — a woman with a fish tail.

"It's a mermaid!" Jonah exclaims.

"It definitely is," she says, squaring her shoulders.

"I thought no one here had ever heard of mermaids," I say.

"They haven't," she says. "But I have. My mother gave this drawing to me. She used to tell me stories about the mermaids all the time."

"Had she seen them?" I ask.

"No," she says. "But my great-great-grandmother Edith did. She was lost at sea and a mermaid saved her. She told my great-grandmother about her mermaid friend, who told my grandmother, who told my mother, who told me. I know everything about them."

"Tell us!" Jonah exclaims.

"They live under the water. In a beautiful kingdom. With streets and houses and restaurants and clothes and everything. The girls are called mermaids and the boys are mermen. And they all have silver tails. And —"

"That's not true," I interrupt. "We saw one. She didn't have a silver tail."

"She must have," Carolyn huffs. "That's what my mother told me. And what my grandmother told her. And what —"

"Did your mom say anything about how to get the mermaids to come on land?" I ask.

"They can't," Carolyn says. "Whenever my great-great-grandmother Edith wanted to see her friend, she had to swim into the sea. The mermaid even gave her a potion that let her breathe underwater for twelve hours."

"Ohhhh," Jonah's eyes light up. "Let's take that! Do you know how to make it?"

I shiver. I am not going underwater with or without a potion, thank you very much. There are sharks underwater. Sharks and other animals that want to eat me.

Carolyn nods. "I do know how to make it, but I can't because one of the ingredients is mermaid spit."

Gross.

"Find me a mermaid," she adds, "and I'll make you the potion."

*   *   *

49

Vivian spots us as we return to the party.

"Where have you been?" she asks.

"Just looking around," I say.

She scowls. "I hope you're not making a mess for me. Russell! Russell, come here!"

A boy about Jonah's age appears at her side. His skin is sun-tanned and freckled. Like everyone else in Mustard, he looks like he spends a lot of quality time on the beach.

"This is my son," Vivian explains. "He can keep you two company. Russell, why don't you show Abby and Jonah where you play tetherball?"

"Let's go sailing instead," the boy says. "I think the royal boathouse is still open."

Yes! That's a great idea. If we're on a boat, we'll be able to find the Little Mermaid. We may not have an underwater potion, but that doesn't mean we can't search the sea.

"No boats!" Vivian snaps. "It's almost dark out, and the sea is too rough."

Oh well.

"I love tetherball," Jonah says.

Russell nods. "Let's go!"

"I'm going to stay here," I say. The last time I played tetherball I almost broke my nose.

Tomorrow, we'll take out a boat. Nothing that will tip over. A rowboat maybe. Then we'll find the Little Mermaid. How hard can it be?

✸ chapter eight ✸

Row, Row, Row Your Rowboat

First thing the next morning, Jonah and I head for the royal boathouse.

We find the yellow hut right on the beach. A suntanned guy in mirrored sunglasses is manning the booth. All around him are different kinds of boats. Windsurfers, sailboats, canoes, banana boats.

"We'd like to borrow a rowboat," I say.

"Of course," the royal boatman says, handing us a ledger. "Just sign one out."

The royal boathouse seems a lot like a library.

"And two life jackets," I add. "And do you happen to have some sort of radio? In case the boat drifts off and we need to get in touch?"

The boatman shakes his head.

"Do you have goggles?" my brother asks.

"Yup, those we got." He reaches under the counter and hands us two pairs.

"What do we need these for?" I ask my brother.

Jonah scrunches his eyebrows as though the answer is obvious. "To look underwater for the Little Mermaid."

"Underwater?" I ask, slightly incredulous. "Are you crazy? We're not going *in* the water."

He snorts. "How else are we going to find her?"

"With our eyes!" I exclaim. "From the boat!"

"That's just silly," he says, taking both pairs of goggles and dangling them from his arm. "We'll swim around."

My mouth gets super dry. "We'll see," I say, but what I really mean is NO WAY.

Jonah turns back to the boatman. "Do you have snorkels? Or scuba equipment?"

"Are those types of boats?" he asks back.

"I guess not," Jonah says.

"You don't know how to scuba," I remind my brother.

My brother shrugs. "Not yet, but I wanna learn."

So not happening.

As we make our way to the shore, I see that half the palace is already out on the water. Including the prince, king, and queen. All three of them are windsurfing.

"Let's take Windsurfers out instead," Jonah begs, his eyes following them with longing. "It looks fun!"

The three royals are being pulled by the wind in all directions. Suddenly, the king flies headfirst into the ocean.

It does not look like fun. It looks terrifying.

"Not a chance," I snap.

"Enjoy," the boatman says as we step into the rowboat and sit side by side. He pushes us out into the water, and off we go.

Five minutes later, sweat is dripping down the sides of my face.

The sun is beating on our heads.

"Push! Pull! Push! Pull!" I order.

It turns out that oars are really heavy. Who knew?

The massive yellow life jackets we're both wearing over our

bathing suits do not help the heat. Between the next push and pull, I catch Jonah trying to take his life jacket off.

"Don't you dare!" I warn.

"But I know how to swim."

"I don't care. You're my baby brother, and it's my job to make sure you don't drown."

We push-pull for another ten minutes before I call out, "Enough." The water is somewhat calm and we're away from the other boats. Might as well stop here. Also, I'm too tired to go on. My arms feel like rubber. I guzzle water from my canteen and motion for Jonah to do the same. I made sure we both filled up before we left. No getting dehydrated on my watch. Still, I feel like there's something I forgot. But what?

Anyway, it's time to find the Little Mermaid. "Oh, Little Mermaid!" I call. " Are you there, Little Mermaid?"

I do not see the Little Mermaid. I just see a lot of blue water.

"We're not going to see her from up here," Jonah says, putting on one of the pairs of goggles. "Let's jump in."

My heart races. "No, Jonah, that is not the plan."

"That's my plan," he says.

"But . . . but . . . but. . . . the water has sharks!"

He stands up and looks like he's ready to cannonball in. "It also has mermaids. And it's not like I'm going to drown. I'm wearing a life jacket."

He swings his arms back and forth.

"Jonah, you're going to flip the boat!"

"I won't," he says. And then he hollers, "Geronimo!" and launches himself over the edge.

Water splashes into my face. "You're so annoying!" I yell.

He ignores me and waves. "Come on in! It's so warm!"

What choice do I have now? I can't let him be in the water by himself. What if he needs me? I hug my life jacket to my chest. At least I can't drown with this on.

I can't, right?

Okay. I can do this. My legs shake as I adjust the goggles on my nose. I carefully — very carefully — dip my big toe in. Anything could be hiding underwater. Not just mermaids. But sharks and stingrays and jelly fish and barracudas and crocodiles, and did I mention sharks?

"Just jump!" Jonah yells. "Don't be such a scaredy-cat!"

My face burns. "I am not a scaredy-cat!"

"You are, too," he says. "You're scared of everything. Sharks. Jumping in the water. Flying by yourself."

"What are you talking about? I'm not afraid of flying by myself."

"So why don't you go see Nana on your own this weekend?"

Is he crazy? "I can't go by myself!"

"Yes you can! My friend Isaac flies by himself once a month. His dad lives in Miami."

I pause. "They let a seven-year-old fly by himself?"

"Yup. He's a UM. Unaccompanied Minor. If he can do it, you can do it."

Flying by myself does sound a *little* scary. What if I got lost at the airport? What if there was turbulence on the plane? "Mom would never let me," I say, my heart hammering.

"It doesn't hurt to ask," he says. "Scaredy-cat."

"I'm not a scaredy-cat!" I snap. And then, before I can change my mind, I jump into the ocean.

I did it! I jumped in! Hurray! Who's a scaredy-cat now, huh? The water is cold. But considering how hot it is outside, it feels good. Really good.

I scream. Something swam by my leg. I take a deep breath. Just a minnow.

I make sure my goggles are on tight, take a deep breath, and peer into the murkiness.

A school of shiny red fish swims by us at top speed. They are very pretty. They are not mermaids.

"Oh, Little Mermaid!" Jonah calls. "Where are you?"

She does not answer.

We watch as all kinds of fish swim by us. Neon-orange ones. Bright-blue ones. A pink one that looks like a balloon with porcupine needles. Lots of fish, but no mermaids.

"We should head back," I say eventually. "This isn't working. We'll have to think of another way." I help Jonah climb into the boat and then heave myself up behind him.

We both drip water everywhere.

"Where are the towels?" Jonah asks, rubbing his wet arms.

Crumbs. I knew I forgot something.

Dejected, we row our way back to the palace.

"I'm hungry," Jonah whines.

"We're almost there," I say. "You can ask Carolyn to make you a grilled cheese."

"I'm not having a grilled cheese without ketchup. That's just sad."

That morning Carolyn made us delicious omelets. And served them with a side of mustard. Jonah had almost started to cry.

"You're crazy," I say.

"Crazy about ketchup," Jonah says.

"Can we focus on rowing, please?" I ask. "The shore is right there! Then I have to figure out a Plan B."

"Maybe she'll come to us," Jonah says.

"Push, Jonah, push! Why would she do that?"

"She loves the prince, right? She probably wants to see him."

"You know," I say, "I think you're right. I remember something in the story about her swimming by the shore and trying to get a glimpse of him. Pull, Jonah, pull!"

"I'm pulling," he snaps. "More than you're pulling."

"I guess we'll have to watch the water as much as we can," I add as the bottom of our boat smashes into the sand.

As we're towing the boat to shore, the queen waves us over to join her for lunch.

"We should change first," I say.

"Don't be silly," she says.

So we join the king, queen, and prince at the oval table outside for lunch. There's a yellow silk tablecloth, and the dishes and silverware are all made of gold. I put my yellow silk napkin on my lap like you're supposed to. I elbow Jonah to do the same.

It seems silly to be so formal when we're all in our bathing suits, but whatever. The king and prince aren't even wearing shirts — they're just in bright-yellow trunks. The queen's swimsuit is pale yellow with a little skirt.

Carolyn serves bowls of squash soup, followed by lemon chicken and yellow rice.

"How was rowboating?" the prince asks while chewing a mouthful of rice. For a prince, he doesn't have the best manners. I'd mention it, but you know. He's a prince. He could probably have me beheaded.

"Hard," I admit. "We were looking for the Little Mermaid, but we didn't find her."

"Ha, ha, ha," they all laugh. "A mermaid! You two are so funny!"

Sigh.

Carolyn gives me a knowing look as she serves me a bowl of banana sorbet.

After lunch, Jonah and I head to our balconies to try to catch a glimpse of the Little Mermaid from there.

Jonah starts to fidget.

"What's wrong?" I ask.

"We don't *both* have to sit here, do we?"

"Why, do you have other plans?"

He smiles sheepishly. "I was going to play with Russell. Wanna come?"

"I have to look for the Little Mermaid!"

"Oh," he says. "Okay."

"If you really want to go, you can," I say, but I don't really expect him to leave me alone.

Jonah jumps up. "Great! I'll see you later!"

I can't help but feel annoyed. He still thinks this is a vacation! We have work to do.

As I stare at the ocean, I wonder if I'm wasting my time. The water is so busy with all the boats and swimmers. We know the Little Mermaid doesn't want to be seen — so then why would she swim close to the surface during the day? She probably does it at night.

I get to my feet. Maybe instead of watching the water, I should spend the day searching the palace grounds for portals to get back home. Make that: *Jonah and I* should spend the day searching the palace grounds.

I find my brother playing Ping-Pong with Russell outside. "Jonah, I need your help. We have to find the portal home." I whisper the last part so Russell doesn't hear. I don't know anything about the kid — I'm not going to trust him with our situation yet.

"Let me just finish this game." Jonah leans over the table and tries to return a shot.

"Jonah! Now!"

"Okay, okay," he grumbles. "Sorry, Russell. Wanna come help us knock on all the furniture to find our way home?"

I purse my lips. I guess we're not keeping our situation a secret.

Russell wrinkles his nose. "Not really. My mom doesn't like when I touch the furniture."

I lead Jonah back inside.

"How great is it that Russell gets to live in the palace?" he asks. "Imagine getting to be here every day."

"Don't get too comfy," I say. "We need to go home eventually. And remember: The portal can be anything. *Any object*."

We step into the main hallway and Jonah looks around. "So it could be a — door?" he asks.

I nod. "Or a mirror. Or a fireplace. Or a table. How are we supposed to know?"

Jonah motions to all the frames on the wall. "Maybe it's a painting."

"Maybe," I say. "Let's try knocking on them to see if any of them make any sounds or start spinning. But don't let them take you yet, 'kay? Stand back."

I start with the full-body portrait of Prince Mortimer. He's wearing his crown and a yellow wet suit. It's really lifelike. His eyes seem to follow me around the room. I knock on the painting three times. It's creepy, but I don't think it's enchanted.

It takes about an hour, but we knock on at least a hundred portraits and paintings.

"Guess it's not the paintings," I say.

"Are we done?" Jonah asks eagerly. "Can I go windsurfing?"

"No, Jonah! We have to check the doors and mirrors."

We hurry around the palace knocking on all of them. We are almost done when —

"Come in!" Vivian yells when we knock on one of the spare bedroom doors.

Oops. "Hi," I say. Inside, I head to the mirror over the dresser and knock three times.

"What in the world are you doing?" Vivian asks, putting down her duster.

I give a small smile. "Um, knocking? See, the way we got here was through a mirror, so a mirror might be our portal home."

"Well, stop it!" she barks. "You're making the frames uneven. Go play outside!"

"I agree," says Jonah.

"Sorry, Vivian," I say. I pull Jonah back downstairs. We're never going to be able to knock on every object in the house. The palace has a lot of stuff. And Vivian is going to kill us.

"What we need," Jonah says, sitting down on a marble step, "is a fairy."

"This story doesn't have a fairy!" I cry. "The only magical person in this story is the sea witch, and we can't go see her since she lives underwater. And I don't happen to have any mermaid spit on me."

"We should try a bat signal."

"Huh?"

"You know how in *Batman* they put up a signal in the sky when they need Batman? That's what we need. A bat signal. But in our case, a mermaid signal."

I'm confused. "For the sea witch?"

"No, for the Little Mermaid. Something to get her to come faster."

"But what would draw the Little Mermaid to us?"

"There's only one thing," Jonah says.

We look at each other and both say it: "Prince Mortimer."

* chapter nine *

The Prince of Portraits

We try to convince Prince Mortimer to hang out on the beach that night, but he says he's too tired from his day of windsurfing. So we use the next best thing we can find.

Prince Mortimer's wet-suit portrait.

We wait until the middle of the night.

Then we sneak downstairs and very, very, very carefully lift Prince Mortimer's portrait up and off the wall.

"Careful!" I whisper as it leans toward Jonah and almost turns my brother into a pancake.

It's a good thing Vivian lives in the basement with Carolyn and the other staff, or she would definitely hear us right now.

"Got it?" I ask. "Lift on three and then we'll carry it out. One! Two! Three!"

We lift. But it's so heavy that we end up dragging it across the foyer and out the back terrace to the sand, as close to the water as we can get.

"Do you really think this is going to work?" Jonah asks when we're finally outside.

"Hopefully the Little Mermaid will see this and want to swim right up to it," I say. "She *is* madly in love with him."

"Unless she hates him now that the story's already different," he says.

"Then all of our problems would be solved," I say. "But I doubt it."

"I just hope she can see it," Jonah says. "I could figure out how to build a fire."

I snort. "You could not."

"I could so," he huffs. "You just need the sun and a piece of glass. How hard could it be?"

"Hard, considering it's the middle of the night."

"Oh, right."

Luckily it's a full moon, so we don't need to rely on my brother's nonexistent fire-starting skills. Everything on the beach is lit up. Including the portrait. Including the water lapping at the base of the portrait. Wetting the paint.

"Quick! Jonah! The prince is losing his feet!"

We hurry to move the portrait back a few feet. I doubt we'd be the royal family's welcome guests if we ruined one of their prized paintings.

"So, what now?" Jonah asks.

"We wait. She'll see the portrait and swim up to us and we'll talk to her. I'll sit behind the painting and hold it up while you keep watch."

At least an hour passes. Jonah's eyes are drooping.

Another hour.

Jonah's eyes are closed.

"Jonah, wake up!" I yell. "I can't do both jobs at once!"

"Not sleeping!" he announces, and opens his eyes wide.

"Let's switch," I say. "That way you can pretend not to sleep while you balance the portrait, and I'll look for her."

We switch. Jonah dozes. I scoop sand from one hand to the other, keeping watch.

When I feel my own eyes start to droop, I decide it's time to call it quits. This is getting us nowhere. I'll give it ten more minutes, and then we're going to —

Splash.

Did I just hear that? Or is it my imagination? I spring to my feet and run closer to the shore.

I see her! I see her! Long green-and-orange tail. Really gorgeous blond hair. It goes down to her waist and is almost the color of butter.

She's treading water by a rock, gazing at the wet-suit portrait of Prince Mortimer.

I want to yell, "Hello!" but I'm afraid of startling her and sending her back under the water. She's not too far out — maybe twenty feet. The water is calm.

If only I could swim out twenty feet. If only I had on a life jacket.

Maybe I can swim out a little. Not too deep. Just to where I can still stand.

Luckily I'm wearing my bathing suit under my sundress. I slip off the dress and wade into the water. Slowly. Carefully. Without making a sound. Without making a splash. Wow, the water is cold at night. I wish *I* had a wet suit.

I almost reach her when the water hits my waist. That's as far as I'm going to go.

"Abby?" Jonah's voice echoes along the beach. "Where are you?"

Uh-oh.

Jonah stands up on the shore, still holding the painting. "Abby!" he yells, blinking the sleep from his eyes. "Where did you go?"

I want to yell, "SHHHH," but I don't want to scare the Little Mermaid.

"Abby! Abby!"

The Little Mermaid sinks her shoulders and tail under the surface.

"Wait!" I cry. "Little Mermaid! Please don't go! We want to help you!"

She disappears under the water.

I lunge toward her. "No! Don't go! We know you love the prince! That's why we brought his painting! To get your attention!" Suddenly my feet no longer touch the ground. Oh, no.

"Abby!" Jonah hollers. "I see her! She's in the water."

"No kidding, Jonah! Can you lend me a hand here, please?"

"You're the girl from the other day, right?" a voice asks timidly. The Little Mermaid! She's talking to me!

"I am," I say, frantically doggy-paddling to stay afloat. "Don't be afraid. We want to help you."

Her face peeks out from behind the rock. "Is that your brother?"

"He definitely is," I say, finally finding the sand with my tiptoes. "You only have sisters, right?"

She nods.

"Lucky." I laugh. "And you're the youngest, huh?"

She nods again and runs her fingers through her wet hair. "How did you know that?" she asks. "Humans never know anything about me."

"Yeah, well, I've read your story. That's what I want to talk to you about. I know that you're a mermaid and that you love the prince and that you want to trade your tail for two legs."

She gasps. "I haven't told anyone that."

"I read it. In a book."

"You know how to read?"

My eyes widen. "You don't?"

Splash. I turn to see Jonah swimming toward us.

The Little Mermaid shakes her head. "No one underwater does. Books and ink don't last underwater. They disintegrate."

That makes sense. "Well, we read. And that's how we know who you are. And what happens to you. And it isn't good."

She pulls on a lock of her hair. "What happens?"

"You go to the sea witch and make a deal with her. She turns your tail into two legs but makes you give her your voice as payment."

She touches her throat. "My voice?"

I nod.

"Your tongue!" Jonah adds, now beside us.

"That's disgusting," the Little Mermaid says.

I agree. "That's why we don't want you to do it."

"Is your name really Little Mermaid?" Jonah asks.

She shakes her head. "It's Lana."

"I'm Jonah," my brother says. "And my sister is Abby."

"Nice to meet you, Abby and Jonah. I've never spoken to humans before."

"We've never spoken to a mermaid before," Jonah says. "Most people here haven't even heard of mermaids. They're weird. They don't use ketchup, either. Is there ketchup where you live?"

It's very late, I'm very cold, and I do not feel like chatting about ketchup. "Lana, let's get back to business. Are we all clear? You can't trade your voice and tail for legs to make Prince Mortimer fall in love with you. It doesn't work. He marries someone else and you end up . . ." My voice trails off. A wave hits me and I struggle to steady myself.

Lana squints. "I end up what?"

"Dead," Jonah says matter-of-factly.

She shivers. "I don't want to be dead."

"Exactly," I agree. "That's why you have to learn to be happy with your life in the water. You get what you get and you don't get upset."

In the moonlight, I see Lana's eyes tear up. "But I don't want to stay where I am! I love Prince Mortimer! And I want to live on land! Where there are sunsets and flying fish!"

"What are flying fish?" Jonah asks.

"You know," she says. "Fish that fly through the air. My sisters told me all about them!"

"You mean birds?" I wonder.

"Flying fish!" she insists. "And shoops!"

"What are shoops?"

"The things you put on your feet. You know — shoops."

"You mean shoes," Jonah says.

She shakes her head. "Shoops!"

"Forget about shoops," I say. "Didn't you hear what I said? You're going to lose everything! Your tongue! Your life! You can't make a deal with the sea witch! You can't give up everything that makes you who you are. It's just not right."

Lana crosses her arms and pouts. Her tail slaps against the water. I guess that's her way of stomping her feet. "But I love him."

She's being ridiculous. "You've never even spoken to him!"

"You don't need to speak to someone to know you love him," she insists. "You don't know what it's like. You're just a kid."

I snort. "You're practically a kid, too."

"I'm fifteen," she huffs.

"That's not even old enough to vote!"

"Vote on what?" she asks.

"The president," I say.

"We don't have presidents here. My father is the king. He runs the ocean. And I'm a princess. And I want to marry the prince."

Jonah floats on his back. "Maybe she could still marry the prince, without making a deal with the sea witch. Maybe they can have a long-distance relationship. Or maybe she can live in the pool. Or he can go live with her in the ocean. He can use the underwater spit potion!"

Lana cocks her head to the side. "There's an underwater spit potion?"

"That's what Carolyn said," I say. "But she hasn't been right about everything. She's the chef at the palace. Apparently her great-great-grandmother met a mermaid."

"I've never heard of a potion," Lana says, "but if it really worked, then the prince could stay with me!"

"Carolyn said it lasted only for twelve hours," Jonah says. "So he'd have to come back on land eventually."

"Maybe we could alternate," Lana says hopefully. "He could spend some time underwater with me, I'll spend some time in his pool . . ."

"It's doable," I say.

"But . . ." Lana hesitates. "Do you think he'll love me even if I'm a mermaid?"

"A guy should love you for who you are," I say. "If you have to change yourself, he's not right for you."

We all nod. Sounds right, doesn't it?

"I like the potion-plus-pool plan," I say. "That way you can still be together without trading anything with the sea witch. I think the prince has to meet you. Once he sees that you're real, and once you tell him that you're the one who saved him from the shipwreck, I'm sure he'll fall in love with you."

"Yeah?" Lana asks.

"Absolutely," I say, and hope that it's true.

✳ chapter ten ✳

The Ocean Can't Hide Everything

the next morning, Jonah, Prince Mortimer, and I head out to the beach, as planned.

"Is she really going to be here?" Prince Mortimer asks.

"Yup. She can't wait to see you again," I say.

Jonah and I told him that the person who swam him to shore is here to see him. We left out the mermaid part, since he didn't believe us the first time we told him. He'll find out the truth soon enough.

My plan is totally going to work. He's going to meet Lana and fall hopelessly in love. So what if she's a mermaid? That won't stop true love! In a few weeks, he'll propose, they'll get married, and — *ta-da!* — happy ending. I glance at my watch. It's only two o'clock back home. We'll get Lana and Prince Mortimer together, and we'll still have five days to find our way back!

We are really getting good at this fairy tale stuff.

As we walk down to the shore, I spot Lana already waiting in the ocean. Her upper body is above the water and her tail is underneath. From this angle, you can't even tell she's a mermaid.

Prince Mortimer's eyes light up. "That's her?"

"Yup," I say.

"She's beautiful." He practically skips all the way down to the water. "Hello!"

She smiles back. "Hello!"

"Are you really the one who saved me from the shipwreck?" he asks.

She nods. "I did. I brought you to Crescent Beach, and then Abby and Jonah pulled you ashore."

"I am forever in your debt," he says, tipping his head. "Come out of the water so we can talk."

"It's so hot out," she says, blushing. "Why don't you come in the water?"

Nice one, Lana!

"I don't have my bathing suit on yet," he says. "Tell me more about how you saved me. You happened to be in the water that night?"

"Yes," she says simply.

"I guess you were on another boat?"

She smiles. "Something like that."

"You have beautiful hair."

"Thank you," she says, batting her eyelashes.

"So you brought me all the way to safety?"

She nods.

His eyes are all shiny and moony. "That's amazing. You saved me, and you're so beautiful."

"Thanks again," she says.

He clears his throat. "Will you marry me?"

Wow, that was fast! I thought it would take a few weeks, but it only took a few minutes. Maybe it really is true love!

Lana's smile lights up her face. "I will!"

"Fantastic," he says, his eyes twinkling. "You will be my princess."

"I should tell you something," she says. "I am already a princess."

Surprise crosses his face. "You are? Princess of where?"

"Of the sea," she says, and with that she dives into the water and shows him her tail.

His face turns white.

Uh-oh.

She reemerges, still smiling.

"You have a t-t-tail!" he spits out.

"I do," she agrees. "I'm a mermaid."

He shakes his head repeatedly. "There is no such thing as mermaids."

Jonah laughs. "Prince Mortimer, she has a tail. You can't argue with that."

The prince waves his hands in front of his face and takes a few steps back. "I can't marry a half person, half fish."

What? No! "Why not?" I ask. "She can sleep in your pool! Or the hot tub! The hot tub is really relaxing!"

He keeps walking back toward his palace. "I just can't! I need a wife who can walk and dance. Someone who can live with me on land. I'm sorry, but this will never work. I take back my proposal!"

"You can't take back a proposal!" I yell.

"Yeah!" Jonah hollers. "Finder's keepers!"

"There's a potion," I tell him. "A potion you can take. You'll be able to live part-time with her under the water."

"There are sharks under the water!" he exclaims. "And I'm not giving up my palace to live in some underwater cave!"

Hmph. What a romantic.

And with that, he turns and storms back to the palace.

"But, but, but . . ." Lana's voice trails off. "I don't live in a cave. My father's palace is just as nice as this palace."

I hurry toward her. "Lana, I'm so sorry."

She winces. "I told you this wouldn't work. I need legs to marry him. And the only way to get them is the sea witch."

"Lana, I don't get it. Why are you so crazy about him? He just insulted your palace! And he's not willing to give anything up for you! Why are you going to give everything up for him?"

She purses her lips. "Because I love him!"

I roll my eyes. I can't help it. She's hopeless. "There has to be another way." I rub my fingers against my temples. "I need to think about it."

"Well, I need legs. I have to go, anyway. My dad is having a party tonight, and I said I'd be there."

"Good." At least a party will keep her from visiting the sea witch. "By tomorrow I'll have another plan. Trust me, I'm very good at planning."

Jonah nods. "She is very good at planning."

"Just whatever you do, don't go to the sea witch. Deal?" I ask.

"Whatever," she says. And then, without even a good-bye, she disappears under the water, leaving me to come up with another plan. Fast.

✴ chapter eleven ✴

That Hurts

Once again, I toss and turn and turn and toss. I can't sleep. Lana is going to come by in the morning, and I have no idea how to get her a happy ending. My only option is to convince her that her current life is super awesome *without* the prince.

And it *so* is. She's a princess! She has great hair! If she lived where we do, she could be in a shampoo commercial. She has five sisters — I wish I had *one* sister, never mind five. Legs just aren't *that* great. I look down at mine. Sure, they can run and dance and stuff. But I've seen her swim, and she moves a lot faster than I do.

There's a loud noise outside the window. It sounds like, "Oooooh!" but it's more of a moaning.

I bet it's quieter underwater. Land has all kinds of creepy sounds.

"Ooooh," I hear again.

Wait. That sounds like a person.

I run out to the balcony and look down at the beach.

"Ooooooooh!" I hear a third time. I look around in the moonlight and eventually see that the sound *is* coming from a person. From Lana. She's lying on the sand.

As I try to figure out what's going on, she starts to flop from side to side. Her tail starts to quiver. And then as I watch, her tail splits right down the middle into two.

OH. MY. GOODNESS.

I have seen a lot of crazy things in fairy tale worlds. But I have never seen anything like this.

I step over the divider and pound on Jonah's balcony door. "Wake up!" I yell. "We have to help her!"

When I turn back to Lana, the green in her legs is slowly fading to the same light color of her skin. Her hair is the same. Her upper body is the same. But now she has legs. LEGS!

And green bikini bottoms.

"What's up?" Jonah asks, opening his balcony door.

"That's what's up!" I say, pointing to Lana. "She made the deal with the sea witch! Why would she do that when I told her not to?" I stomp my right foot. I am mad. So very mad.

"Oooohhhh!" Lana moans.

"We need to help her," I say. "Get a towel."

We hurry down to the beach and find her still twisting in pain on the sand.

"Does it hurt?" Jonah asks her.

"Obviously, it hurts!" I exclaim. "She wouldn't be making those sad sounds if it didn't hurt!"

Lana just nods.

I put my hands on my hips. "Did you go to the sea witch?"

She nods again.

"Why would you do that?" I wonder. "I told you *not* to!"

She opens her mouth to say something but then immediately closes it.

I gasp in horror. Since she has legs and went to the sea witch . . . the sea witch has her . . . has her . . . has her tongue. "Did you give her your . . . ?" I can't even say the word. It's too gross.

Lana nods. But then she points to her legs.

My stomach churns. She really did it. Gave away her tongue for legs. Why would she do that? Why would anyone do that?

I take a deep breath. I take the towel from a very wide-eyed Jonah and wrap it around her wet shoulders. "Can you stand?" I ask.

She shrugs, which I take to mean *I don't know*. Communicating with someone with no tongue is *not* going to be easy. She holds my hands, and I gently lift her up.

She's shaky on her feet, but it seems to work. At the same time, she grimaces, so I guess it hurts. After a few seconds, she is able to walk on her own.

We take her back to the palace.

I want to yell at her. To tell her that she made a huge mistake.

But by the pained look on her face, I think she already knows it.

"Come sleep in my suite," I tell her. "We'll deal with this in the morning."

She looks like she wants to say something, but then just nods. Without a word, she follows me to my room.

✳ chapter twelve ✳

Nice to Meet You Again

Lana is up before I am. She's sitting on the floor of my room, examining her toes.

"How are you feeling?" I ask.

She gives me a big smile and a thumbs-up.

She motions to her body. I have no idea what she's trying to say.

She motions again.

"You're cold?"

She shakes her head.

"Hot?"

She tugs on the yellow nightie I lent her last night. Maybe she's saying thank you.

"You're welcome," I tell her.

She shakes her head again and then makes a waving motion with her hands.

"You want to go swimming?"

Her cheeks turn red and she stomps her foot. She pulls at the nightie again and grunts.

"Oh, you want to get dressed!"

She gives me a big nod. Then she makes a show of patting down her hair.

"You want to wash your hair and then get dressed and then see Prince Mortimer?"

She claps. I guess I got it.

The door bursts open. "Who are you?" Vivian looks at Lana and demands.

Lana's eyes widen in fear. She opens her mouth to answer but then seems to remember she can't say anything.

"She's a mermaid!" I say. "Remember I told you I was looking for a half fish, half human?"

Vivian clucks her tongue. "She doesn't look like she's half fish. She has legs."

Good point. "Well, she used to be half fish," I say.

"I don't approve of lying, Miss Abby," Vivian says. "Does your friend with legs have any clothes, or did she lose her luggage, too?"

I shake my head. "No luggage."

"I'll call the tailor," Vivian barks.

Twenty minutes later, Lana has been measured and has showered and is wearing a brand-new sleeveless yellow sundress. She still smells a little salty, but I guess that's what happens when you live most of your life in the ocean.

"Now get outside, both of you, so I can clean," Vivian orders.

Through the balcony window, we spot Prince Mortimer already out on the beach, standing by the royal boathouse. Jonah is up, too — he and Russell are building sandcastles.

Prince Mortimer looks up, and Lana waves at him.

Prince Mortimer waves back and gives Lana a slightly quizzical look.

Lana curtsies. Then she pulls my hand and hurries me outside.

Prince Mortimer watches us as we approach.

"Hi," I say. "Do you remember Lana? She gave up her tail to be with you, so I hope you're happy." I don't mean to sound as grumpy as I do, but I guess I can't help it. I feel grumpy.

"You have legs!" the prince exclaims.

She blushes and nods.

"She gave up her voice for those legs," I say.

Lana gives me a sour look.

What? She did! Lana should be thanking me. In the original story, the Little Mermaid had no translator, and the prince never knew that she was the one who saved him and he ended up marrying someone else. The only reason he knows what's going on here is because of me.

And maybe Jonah. My brother who is currently making snow angels in the sand.

Mostly me.

"Who cares about your voice?" the prince exclaims. "You look gorgeous."

I have no choice but to roll my eyes.

He takes Lana's hand and twirls her around. Then he drops to one knee. "I will honor my earlier proposal. Will you marry me?"

She nods happily.

Lana and the prince embrace. Everyone on the beach — the king, queen, Jonah, Russell, and the guy manning the royal boathouse — claps and cheers.

And me? Honestly, I'm not sure how I feel. On the one hand, I'm happy that Lana got what she wanted. She wanted to marry the prince, and now she will. She's getting her happy ending.

But on the other hand, she:

1. Lost her tail!
2. Lost her voice!
3. Lost her underwater kingdom! Will she ever even see her family again?
4. Is marrying a guy who only likes her for her legs!

Even though she seems happy, I can't help feeling sad.

The prince takes Lana's hand. "We'll get married immediately. Three days from now. We'll do it in the ballroom, of course."

Of course? I had so expected him to stay on the beach.

Lana follows him into the palace. For someone who just got legs, she looks very glamorous as she walks.

"See?" Jonah says, running up to me, covered in sand. "It all worked out."

"Not all of it," I say. I can't shake the sad feeling.

"So now what?"

"I guess we go home."

"Already?" He looks longingly at the water. "Don't you think we should stay a few more days? Just until the wedding? That way we can make sure Lana gets married and has her happy ending. What time is it at home?"

I glance at my watch. "Three A.M."

"Great!" he cheers. "Then we have four hours until Mom and Dad wake us up. Which is four days. I'm going kayaking."

I grab his arm before he runs away. "We need to look for the portal!"

"We will, we will," he says. "How about we split up?"

"All right," I say. "That sounds reasonable."

He scrunches his nose. "You go check the furniture," he says.

"We already checked the mirrors. I guess I can check the tables and chairs. What are you checking?" I'm glad he's finally willing to do some work.

As he runs toward the beach, he calls over his shoulder, "I'm going to check all the kayaks!"

I walked right into that one.

✳ chapter thirteen ✳

Lost in Translation

t he next day, we're in the dining room having tea and discussing wedding details.

Chef Carolyn can't stop staring at Lana. "She's really a mermaid?" she asks, eyes wide.

"She was, but she gave it up," I explain.

"I wish she could talk! I have so many questions!"

The prince clears his throat. "Back to the menu," he says. "Chef Carolyn, I'd like you to prepare sole, tilapia, and yellowfin tuna. Fish, in honor of my little mermaid!"

Lana's eyes widen to the size of her teacup.

"What's wrong, my pet?" Prince Mortimer asks, patting her knee. "You don't like tuna?"

She shakes her head frantically.

"What about sole?"

More head shaking.

"Then what would you like to serve?" he asks.

She shakes her head no, and then makes a weird squiggly motion with her hands.

"She doesn't want fish. She must want lobster. Perfect!" He kisses her on the forehead, gets up, and leaves the room.

Lana's eyes fill with tears.

"Did you not want lobster?" I ask.

She shakes her head.

"Wait, I'm confused," Jonah says. "You did want lobster or you didn't?"

She shakes her head again.

"Which one?"

Lana drops her head down on the table and sighs.

What can I say? It's tough to talk without a voice.

Since they got engaged, the prince and Lana don't seem to understand each other at all. Lana does a lot of nodding and shaking her head, but it's tough to answer questions like: What do you want to serve for dinner? You can't answer that with a nod or a head shake.

Vivian hurries into the living room clutching a paper card. "Look," she calls out. "The calligrapher just finished the wedding invitations. Don't they look nice?" She places one in Lana's hands. "I'll send one to your family."

Lana shakes her head. I notice that her eyes fill with tears but that she blinks them away.

"You're not inviting your dad?" I ask, shocked.

She shakes her head again.

Communicating would be so much easier if mermaids knew how to read and write.

"What about your sisters?" I ask. "Aren't they going to be your bridesmaids?"

She points to me.

"Me?" I ask. "You want me to be your bridesmaid?"

She nods.

Wow! I've never been a bridesmaid before. But I've always, always, ALWAYS wanted to! The dress! The bouquet! I don't know what else bridesmaids do, but I'm sure it's fun.

"I accept!" I cheer. "I'm going to be an amazing bridesmaid. The best bridesmaid ever. But wait — if I'm the only bridesmaid, does that make me the maid of honor?"

Lana nods.

This is the most exciting thing that has ever happened to me. Besides falling into fairy tales through my magical mirror, obviously.

I am going to be *the* Little Mermaid's maid of honor! Who else can say that? No one! Only me! "But are you sure you don't want to ask your sisters?"

She shakes her head and looks down at the invitation.

"Read it out loud!" Jonah says.

I shoot him a look across the table.

He blushes. "Oh, right. I keep forgetting you can't talk."

"She can't read, either," I say. A lightbulb goes off in my head. "I have an idea! An idea that's going to fix everything. Okay, not everything, but definitely your communication problems."

Lana looks up at me eagerly.

I wait for Jonah to make a drum roll or something, but when none comes I turn to Lana and announce, "I'm going to teach you to write! If you can write, then you'll be able to communicate with Prince Mortimer. And with everyone. Then you won't be so frustrated. When anyone asks you a question you can just write the answer down!"

"Great idea, Abby," Jonah says. "I think I'll go play tennis while you do that. Russell is having his tutoring lessons now, but maybe I can get him to sneak away."

I sigh.

Lana points to the invitation.

I don't understand what she wants. "You want me to read it to you?"

She shakes her head no. She nods. She shakes her head no again. She points to herself and then her eyes and then the invitation.

"I think she wants you to teach her to *read*, too," Jonah says.

"Of course! Reading and writing go hand in hand." I square my shoulders. "Just call me Professor Abby." All I need now is a pair of eyeglasses and a blazer. Oh, and pencils. And paper. "Jonah, before you disappear for the day, please find me some paper and pencils."

Jonah hurries off. When he comes back with paper and different-colored pencils, I spread them all out on the table.

Pencils, check! Paper, check!

Now what? I've never actually taught anyone to read before. Where do I start?

"Okay, bye!" Jonah calls.

"Wait! Jonah. You just learned to read, right?"

"Right," he says. "This year."

"Can you, um, tell me how to start?"

He fidgets with the door. "How about with A?"

I nod. "So we'll go through all the letters, and I'll teach Lana the sounds. Thanks. You can go now."

Jonah bolts out the door.

I write a capital A. No need to confuse her with small letters yet. "A makes an 'ahhhh' sound. Ahhh!" I overemphasize. "Also, sometimes 'ay.' A is for . . . 'Abby'! That's me. A is also for 'at' and 'animal.' Why don't I write it down and then you copy it?"

I write a big A, and then she copies it ten times.

I smile. "A is for 'awesome.' Now let's do B. Do you know what B is for?"

She shakes her head.

"B is for 'brother,'" I say. "And 'ballroom.' And best of all, 'bridesmaid.'"

✶ chapter fourteen ✶

Read It and Weep

Lana is a fast learner. By the end of the day, she knows the whole alphabet. By the day before the wedding, she can pretty much read and write.

It helps that we recruit Russell's tutor. I'll admit it: I'm no reading and writing expert. But it was all my idea, so I'm taking credit for it anyway, thank you very much.

Lana decides not to tell Prince Mortimer what she's up to. She wants it to be a surprise. Since he's always outside surfing, canoeing, or windsurfing, it hasn't been much of a problem.

When Lana takes breaks, we are very busy with wedding prep. We go to dress fittings with the palace tailor. Lana's dress is the perfect bride's dress — white, strapless, and fitted on top, with a big, poofy skirt. My maid-of-honor dress has capped sleeves, a sweetheart neckline, and a short skirt. It's pretty gorgeous — and yellow, of course.

Also, as maid of honor, it is my job to help Lana prepare for her big march down the aisle. I make her practice walking. Heel-toe, heel-toe, heel-toe. I read a book about a model once, and that's how she was told to walk down the catwalk. I'm guessing it's the same for a wedding.

I even practice my own walking — as maid of honor I have to make sure not to trip.

Being maid of honor is pretty important, you know. And time-consuming.

My job is to keep Lana happy and worry-free all day. Also to get an updo, manicure, and pedicure on the morning of the wedding. Yup, the bride and the maid of honor both get their hair and nails done! I've never had an updo, manicure, or pedicure, so I'm psyched.

Now, the day before the wedding, while Lana studies with Russell's tutor, I try and find the portal home. I knock on everything I see. Bedposts. Bowls. Stairs. Nothing works.

Jonah is supposed to be helping, but he's too busy vacationing.

"Can you please help me?" I ask him, finding him doing handstands in the pool.

"Abby, I'm sure it will be something at the wedding. The portal usually pops up at the *end* of our adventure."

"Jonah, of course it pops up at the end of our adventure! Once we find it, we leave!"

"Not true," he says, floating on his back. "We wait until the happy ending is all straightened out, and then we leave. The happy ending here isn't all straightened out yet."

"It practically is," I tell him.

"Then I'm sure we'll figure it out tomorrow," he says. "Why don't you come swimming?"

"Just because you're taking a break doesn't mean I can," I huff. Although it is very hot. And the pool does look very refreshing. But also deep. Anyway, I have other things to do.

I leave my brother to feel guilty in the pool while I go check on Lana.

She's scribbling on a piece of paper. She's writing! My plan totally worked!

"What are you writing?" I ask.

She takes a clean piece of paper and writes, "RITING PRESINT FOR PRINS."

Okay, so she's not the best speller yet, but come on. Two days ago she didn't even know that her name started with the letter L. Give her a break.

"Cool," I say.

She nods. Her cheeks are flushed with happiness.

"What is it?"

She points her pencil at her notebook.

It says:

"ONCE UPON A TIME THER WAS A MERMAD PRINCES. ON HER 15 BIRTHDA SHE SAW A PRINS FAL IN THE WATER —"

"Oh!" I squeal. "It's the story of how you met!"

She nods.

"He's going to be so impressed," I say. "Wait, Lana, I want to ask you a question. How come you don't want to invite your family to the wedding?"

She sighs. She pulls out a fresh piece of paper and writes, "THEY CANT COM ON LAND. AND THEY MUST

BE VERE MAD AT ME. AND NOT FEEL LIKE CELEBRATING."

"Are you sure? We could send them the invite — you never know what they might say."

"NO," she writes. "THEY CANT REED."

Oh, right.

That's so sad! She seems to think so, too, because I catch her frowning and gazing toward the window that overlooks the water.

On the bright side: I'm still the maid of honor!

✳ chapter fifteen ✳

Your Bed Has Been Made

*t*hat night we all eat together in the dining room.

It's a pretty delicious dinner. Chef Carolyn makes a barbeque. There are cheeseburgers and corn and grilled salami. Of course, there's mustard. For dessert we have banana pie and lemon cake. These people really know how to eat, even if most of the food is yellow.

During dessert, Lana stands up and hands a box to Prince Mortimer. There's a yellow ribbon tying it closed.

"What's this?" he asks.

She smiles.

"It's her wedding gift to you," I explain, not wanting to give away the surprise but bursting with excitement. How amazing is she that she learned to write in two days? She's amazing! And it was all my idea! I am the best maid of honor ever!

Prince Mortimer unwraps the ribbon, opens the box, and takes out pretty papers laced together with ribbon. The first page reads: *Our Story, by Princess Lana.*

"How nice," the prince says before placing it beside his plate. He goes right back to his lemon cake.

Lana looks shocked.

I *feel* shocked. "Aren't you going to read it?"

"I'm in the middle of dessert," he explains, taking another forkful. "Yum."

Lana's face falls.

No. No, no, no. "But don't you see what a big deal this is? Lana wrote that! Herself! She learned to read and write so you guys can communicate!"

Prince Mortimer takes a big gulp of pineapple juice before continuing. "What does Lana need to read and write for? She's a princess. She just needs to smile, dance, and be beautiful."

I drop my fork and it clatters against my plate.

Jonah's jaw drops open.

Lana gasps. She looks at Prince Mortimer and then back at me. She shakes her head. Then she pushes her chair back and runs out of the room.

Everyone else at the table shrugs.

"Guess she doesn't like lemon cake," the prince says, and continues eating. "You know what we should have at the wedding? Lemon meringue pie."

I can't listen to one more minute of this. I excuse myself from the table and hurry after Lana. I do kind of hope they have lemon meringue pie at the wedding, though. I love lemon meringue pie.

When I walk into her room, just down the hall from mine, she is pacing.

"Sorry about that," I say.

Lana throws her arms up in the air. She picks up a paper and pen and writes, "I THINK I MAD A BIG MISTAK!!!"

I think she made a big mistake, too. Which I told her from the beginning. Not that I'm going to say "I told you so" now. Even though I really want to.

But I won't.

Her eyes tear up, and she continues writing:

"I GAVE UP EVERETHING TO BE HERE. MY FAMI-LIE. MY HOME. MY VOICE. MY SISTERS!! MY DAD! OH MY POOR DAD."

"What's wrong with your dad?" I ask. "Isn't he the king?"

She nods. "HE IS LONELLY SINCE MY MOM DIED 10 YEARS AGO."

Her poor dad. First he lost his wife, and now he pretty much lost his daughter. I sit down on her perfectly made bed. I'm impressed. She makes a good bed.

"WHAT SHUD I DO?"

As I glance down at the bed, I remember one of my mom's favorite expressions. "You made your bed, and now you have to sleep in it," I say.

She shakes her head and then writes, "VIVIAN MADE MY BED!"

Oh. Right. She probably made Jonah's, too. I, on the other hand, made my own bed, thank you very much. Anyway, that's not the point. "It's an expression," I say. "What I mean is, I'm not sure what you *can* do except get married." And this isn't because of the maid of honor thing. I swear. "You can't go back to your family. You don't have a tail. Can you swim in the ocean the way you are now?"

She shakes her head no.

"And, anyway, if you cancel the wedding, he'll marry some-one else. And then . . ." my voice trails off.

And then.

Although maybe the deal with the sea witch changed. It's possible, isn't it? Since the story has changed? "Did the sea witch tell you that if the prince marries someone else you'll . . . you'll . . . stop living the next morning?" I can't bear to say the word *die*.

She nods.

Crumbs.

We can't let that happen. No matter what.

✳ chapter sixteen ✳

On the Other Hand

It's W-day. Wedding day.

And M-day: Maid-of-honor day.

Also, G-day: Go-home day. Assuming we can find the portal. My watch says it's just before six, so technically we have until tomorrow, but I don't want to be late.

I spend the morning in the royal salon getting ready. When they wash my hair with yummy lemon-scented shampoo and conditioner, I lean back and admire the gold chandelier above my head. Then they set my hair in curlers, and while it dries, they place my feet in a little claw-foot tub for a warm pre-pedicure foot bath.

Ahhhh.

Even more melty than a hot tub, if you can believe it.

They file and paint my toes gold. Then they do the same to my fingernails.

It's all very glamorous. I feel like Dorothy in *The Wizard of Oz* when she's getting all prettied up before she meets the wizard.

Lana and the queen are both in the royal salon, too.

Lana doesn't say much. Obviously, she can't talk. She doesn't write much, either, though. She just stares into the distance, looking miserable.

On the other hand, the queen doesn't *stop* talking.

"Everyone is coming," she says. "Even the royal family of Watermelon will be here. They're bringing their lovely daughter Alison. Lana, darling, she's about your age and goes to school here in Mustard. I hope you two will become friends."

Lana just shrugs.

A pretty princess named Alison? I can't help but wonder if that's the girl Prince Mortimer marries in the original story. Whatever. She's not marrying him in *this* story.

And: Watermelon? Really?

Once my nails are dry, my hair is arranged in a very cool and elaborate updo, with gold barrettes to keep it in place. They even sprinkle in gold sparkles to make it shine. Then they get to work on my makeup.

Makeup!

I've used some of my mom's blush before, just for fun, but I've never gotten my *makeup* done. They use pink blush! And gold eye shadow! And mascara! And pink lip gloss! By the time they're done, I look years older. At least thirteen.

Lana is still getting her makeup done, so I tell her I'll meet her in her suite in half an hour to help her get dressed.

One hour until the wedding!

The people around the palace are buzzing and hopping and getting everything ready. I peek into the ballroom to see what it looks like, and there are at least a hundred gold chairs set up with an aisle down the middle.

I practice my wedding walk all the way back to my room. Heel-toe, heel-toe. Slow and steady. I try to keep my shoulders down like my nana always tells me to.

I miss my nana. She would be so proud to know that I'm *the* Little Mermaid's maid of honor.

I change into my yellow maid-of-honor dress in my room, and then hurry over to Lana's door to see how she's doing. I knock once. Twice. Three times. I can hear her inside, but she's not answering.

Oh, right. She can't talk.

Finally she throws open the door.

She's in her full veil and wedding gown. Her hair hangs loose and curly around her shoulders. She looks gorgeous. Sure, she always looks gorgeous, but now she looks *extra* gorgeous. Like a princess. Like a *real* princess. No — like a fairy tale princess.

"You look beautiful," I breathe.

She shrugs.

Then I notice her face.

Her eyes are wide, her skin is pale, and she's biting her lower lip so hard, I think it might be bleeding. She also has her right hand wound through her hair and appears to be pulling on it. Hard. She looks terrified.

"Lana, you don't look so good. I mean, you look gorgeous, but you also kind of look like you're about to barf."

Just what every bride wants to hear on her wedding day. Maybe I'm not the world's best maid of honor, after all.

Lana closes her eyes and then opens them again, looking even sicker.

I'm not sure what to do. Or what to say. As maid of honor, it's my job to make her feel better. To get her to the altar. But how can I convince her to go through with a wedding when she's so clearly unhappy? On the other hand, if she doesn't marry Prince Mortimer, what will happen to her? Nothing good. Something bad, in fact.

Someone pounds on the door. "Guys, it's me! Jonah! Can I come in?"

"Yup," I say, nervously watching Lana.

"Everyone's waiting," he says, waltzing in. "Are you two ready?"

Jonah looks adorable. He's in a black tux with a mustard-colored bow tie. I wish I had a camera to take a picture and show my parents. Although then they would wonder why we were at a fancy event without them. It might be hard to explain.

Lana takes a deep breath. Then she nods. She marches out of the room, and we trail behind her. She'll be happy, right? This will all work out.

It has to work out. Has to, *has* to, HAS to.

And the pit of fear in my stomach has to go away.

We follow Lana down the stairs and toward the ballroom. For some reason, this feels more like a funeral march than a wedding. Maybe that's just how weddings always are? It's not like I've ever been in one before. What do I know?

Vivian is waiting for us at the bottom. "You look beautiful, Princess Lana! You, too, Abby. Take your bouquets." She hands us both bunches of yellow roses and white baby's breath, tied together with gold ribbon.

Ohhhh, pretty.

Jonah waves to us and slips inside so he can sit down with the rest of the crowd.

I peek through the open doors and see that the room is packed with at least a hundred people. Prince Mortimer is also in a black tuxedo and a mustard-colored bow tie, and he's already at the altar. Yellow flowers are everywhere — roses, tulips, daisies, and other kinds that I don't know the names of. The room looks really beautiful. I can't believe they put this all together in three days. It must be a world record.

Violin music begins to play.

"Abby," Vivian says. "You're first. Then Lana."

My turn! I look back at Lana. "You're okay?"

She nods and motions for me to go.

I don't want to leave her by herself, but I guess that's my job. I take a step. Heel-toe, heel-toe, heel-toe. I'm doing it! I'm doing it! This is fun! I am *so* acing this. Heel-toe, heel-toe, heel-toe! I did it! I made it the whole way without tripping!

When I get the altar, the prince is smiling at me.

I smile back. Maybe he's not so bad. He loves her, right? He'll make her happy?

He is smiling at me, right? I look behind me and realize he's actually smiling at his reflection in the stained-glass window.

Hrm. Well, at least he's smiling. Smiling's still good, right? He could be frowning at his reflection. That would be worse.

I look up and spot Lana, waiting at the doors.

Everyone stands up and turns to her.

She really does look stunning. She only looks a little bit like she's going to barf, and I'm probably the only one who notices.

The violinist begins to play the "Here Comes the Bride" march.

Lana doesn't move. She just stares. And stares.

Uh-oh. I motion for her to come.

She stares some more. She pulls her hair. She takes one step forward.

She takes one step back.

And then another step back. Then she spins on her heels and runs the other way.

✳ chapter seventeen ✳

Better Now Than Later

A rumble goes through the room.

The prince looks at me in surprise. "Did she just leave?"

"Um . . ." It definitely seems like she did. "Maybe she had to pee or something?"

"She couldn't have waited until after the wedding?"

"A girl's gotta go when she's gotta go," I say, not really believing that:

1. I'm talking to a prince about pee or
2. Lana actually had to pee.

"Why don't I go see what the issue is?" I say nervously. And then, without waiting for a response, I hurry back down the aisle — no time for heel-toe now — and run out of the ballroom.

Should I really check the bathrooms? I realize there's no need to, because as soon as I step out of the ballroom, I see that the front door is wide open.

Lana left the palace. She's officially a runaway bride.

I run right after her and spot her already at the shore, holding up her dress, up to her knees in the water.

"What are you doing?" I ask. "You're supposed to be getting married!"

She shakes her head.

"You're not getting married?"

She shakes her head again.

"But what about the prince?"

More shaking.

"But you know what this means! If he marries someone else, you'll die!"

Her eyes fill with tears and she nods.

I pace up and down the sand. This is not good. Not good at all. If the prince does marry someone else, she's in serious trouble. We're all in serious trouble, because that's not a happy ending at all. That's a terrible ending. That's the same ending as the original ending! I take a deep breath and try to calm down. It's not like he's going to marry someone else *today*. We have some time to figure this out. Maybe the prince will learn to be less of a jerk and she'll change her mind. Maybe we can find another prince that she would want to marry, and *that* would work instead.

I hear Jonah's voice from the palace door. "Abby! What's happening?"

I guess I have to tell them the wedding's off. Had I known that canceling a wedding would be part of my maid-of-honor duties, I might not have been so excited about the job. "You stay here," I say finally. "Don't go in the water. I don't want you drowning. I'm going to talk to Prince Mortimer."

She closes her eyes in relief and I slowly make my way back to the palace.

Everyone looks up at me as I enter the ballroom.

"She better be coming now," Prince Mortimer barks. His face is bright red. He looks furious.

"Um, I don't think she is," I say timidly from about halfway down the aisle.

"Darling, how long will she be?" the queen asks, checking her gold wristwatch.

"A pretty long time," I say. "I think she wants to . . ." I have to just say it. "I think she wants to cancel the wedding."

Several hundred gasps echo through the room. I wince.

"You're kidding!"

"Cancel the wedding?"

"Not marry the prince?"

"Is she *crazy*?"

Prince Mortimer's face falls. "I can't believe she would do that to me," he cries, looking genuinely pained.

As insensitive as he's been, I can't help but feel bad for him. No one wants to be left at the altar.

The queen jumps up. "How dare she run off like that!"

The king stands up beside her and turns to the crowd. "Dudes, we know you all came to see a royal a wedding today, and we *will* have a royal wedding today. Morty, there must be someone else here that you could marry."

My heart stops. What? Is he kidding? He must be kidding.

The queen nods. "Yes! Princess Alison is here today. Morty, would you marry her?"

"Let me see her," Prince Mortimer says.

The queen motions to Princess Alison. "Sweetie, will you stand up, please?"

Princess Alison stands up and curtsies. She has tight spiral curls and looks familiar. I know! She's the girl from the school, the one who got help after we found Prince Mortimer on Crescent Beach! She's the princess of Watermelon? Not surprisingly, she's wearing a satiny red dress, with a green sash and green shoes.

The prince nods. "I'll marry her. I like her hair. She's pretty."

The king claps. "Fantastic. Alison, would you like to marry our son?"

"Yeah, okay," she says, twisting a curl around her finger and snapping her chewing gum. "He *is* cute."

"And your parents? The king and queen of the kingdom of Watermelon? Do you agree to this union?"

"We do!" the king says, a big, smug smile on his face, a red-and-green checkered bow tie around his neck.

This isn't happening. THIS ISN'T HAPPENING.

"This isn't happening!" I yell.

Jonah tugs on my arm and whispers, "I'm pretty sure it *is* happening."

"Great," Prince Mortimer says. "Let's start the music over.

Do you want to do the whole walk-down-the-aisle thing, or just come up?"

"I'll just come up," Princess Alison says. She maneuvers her way through the crowd, fluffs her dress, and begins walking down the remainder of the aisle. "Excuse me," she says to Jonah and me as she squeezes past us.

"What a perfect match," a woman sitting near us says. "She's a princess, he's a prince. He's handsome, and she's beautiful. They go together like French fries and mustard!"

"What is wrong with you people?" I shriek. "Mustard does not go on French fries! Ketchup goes on French fries! Ketchup! Or mayonnaise, in some countries. Or maybe a mixture of the two, if you're into that. But not mustard! Never mustard!"

Everyone stares at me.

Am I losing it?

"I totally agree," Jonah says. "C'mon, Abby, let's go. We need to help Lana."

Yes, we definitely need to help her. Because Prince Mortimer is marrying someone else, which means that Lana is going to DIE in the morning.

Unless we can save her.

✳ chapter eighteen ✳

Night Swimming

We find Lana sitting on the sand, staring sadly into the sunset.

"You need to go talk to the sea witch," I tell her. Lana needs to convince the witch to reverse the spell.

She points to her mouth and then her chest.

"You can't breathe underwater," I say.

She nods.

"Any way we can get the sea witch to come ashore?" I ask.

Lana shakes her head and shimmies her hand so it looks like a tail.

"She doesn't have legs," I confirm. "But she's a witch; she can do whatever she wants."

"She probably doesn't want to come on land," Jonah says. He can be annoyingly logical.

Argh! We have to fix this! We're running out of time!

"Maybe Princess Alison won't *really* marry Prince Mortimer," Jonah says. "Maybe she'll pull a Lana, and bolt at the last minute."

Just then we hear loud clapping inside the palace and choruses of "Congratulations!"

"There goes that idea," I mumble.

"Oh! Oh!" Jonah shrieks. "What about that potion Carolyn talked about? Remember? The one that her great-great-grandmother used to go underwater? The spit potion?"

I shake my head. "Do you think that even works?"

"Well, she should try it. What other choice do we have?"

He has a point.

We find Carolyn in the kitchen, slicing lemons.

"Remember that potion you said your great-great-grandmother used to go underwater?" I ask.

"How could I forget?" she says with a laugh.

"Do you know how to make it?"

"Do I remember the ingredients? Of course I do. Mermaid's spit, a tablespoon of sea salt, three fish eggs, a tablespoon of water, a teaspoon of club soda, and a pinch of algae. I've always wanted to make it, but finding the mermaid's spit has been difficult."

"We have the spit," I say. "We need some potion so Lana can go underwater."

"Of course," she says, putting down her knife. "Anything for my favorite mermaid."

She gathers all the stuff from the kitchen, mixes it up in a glass, and then runs with us outside and hands the glass to Lana. Lana spits inside, then takes a sip. Then she turns and hurries into the ocean, diving underwater. Two seconds later she pops up, gasping and shaking her head.

"I guess it doesn't work," I say.

"Maybe now that Lana has legs, her spit isn't mermaid-y anymore," Carolyn says.

Lana leans over and carves into the sand: "I DON'T HAVE A TAIL BUT I WILL ALWAYS BE A MERMAID."

"In that case," Jonah says, "maybe a mermaid can't use her own spit. Or maybe the spell only works on humans."

"Lana's a human," I say.

Carolyn shakes her head. "She's a mermaid. She just said so herself."

Jonah tugs on my hand. "You know what that means, right? It might work on us."

Huh? "Us?"

"Us," he repeats. "We're human."

"*I* am, yes. I'm not always so sure about you."

"Seriously, Abby. *We'll* try the potion."

"I doubt it will work," I say, my heart hammering.

"I bet it will," he says. "We'll get to breathe underwater! It'll be fun!"

"Sharks. Waves. Salt in our mouths. That doesn't sound like fun. And it's going to be dark soon. How will we see anything?" I can't do it. I just can't.

"Don't you have a light on your watch?" he asks.

"Yeah." As if one probably-waterproof-watch light is enough for me to go up against the entire ocean.

"Let's just try. It's our only chance."

"Are there any other options?" I ask, my voice squeaky. "There must be. Maybe Carolyn wants to try it?"

Carolyn shakes her head. "Me? Are you crazy? I eat shark. I don't let them eat me!"

"You eat shark?" Jonah asks, eyes wide.

She nods. "I'll make it for you. It's delicious."

"No thanks," we say in unison.

Jonah looks at me. "I think it's up to us, then. Let's do it!"

Goose bumps cover my whole body. He wants me to go underwater. No life jacket. No air.

I can't. I can't. I can't.

I *have* to.

Slowly I nod.

Lana hands Jonah the cup.

"Cheers!" Jonah cries, and takes a big sip. "It tastes like sushi!"

I roll my eyes. "Have you ever even had sushi?"

"No, but I bet this is what it tastes like. It could use some ketchup." When Jonah's done, he hands me the cup and scurries toward the water, diving right in.

"Wait, Jonah!" I yell, but it's too late. He's under.

He pops up. "It works! It really works!"

"Great. Just, um, great!" My hands shake. Before I sip, I ask, "But how will we ever find the sea witch?"

"Lana can make us a map," Jonah calls.

Carolyn takes a pen and paper out of her apron and hands it to Lana. "Here you go."

Lana starts to sketch. When she's done, she writes "2 HOURS" on top.

"It'll take us two hours to get there?" I ask.

Lana nods.

That's a long time for us to be swimming. Two hours to the sea witch's place, two hours back, plus how long to convince the witch to help us? At least we have twelve hours to work with.

"Bottoms up," Carolyn says.

I nod, and then I swallow a gulp of the potion. I almost gag. But I keep swallowing because I have to.

P.S. My brother's not wrong — a little ketchup *would* go a long way.

I hand Lana the glass and then carefully wade into the water. The *dark* water. This can't be a good idea. I barely swim well during the day; how am I going to swim well at night?

"Just dunk!" Jonah orders me.

I bristle at being bossed around by my baby brother, but I know he's right. Getting into the water is like taking off a Band-Aid. It always hurts less to just rip it off. I'm in up to my waist. I should go under now.

Okay, *now.*

"Time is ticking," Jonah calls. "I'm going under again!"

"Jonah, hold on!" I yell, but then he disappears under the surf. At first I see bubbles rise to the surface but then they stop.

I don't like bubbles that stop. My heart feels like it might pound out of my chest.

Now I have no choice. I grip the map in my hand, hold my nose with the other, seal my eyes shut, and go under.

Cold, cold, cold! I carefully open my left eye. At first it's blurry, but then it clears up. This is a hopeful sign. It doesn't sting or anything. I open the right eye.

Around me I see blue. Lots and lots of navy blue. I'm glad the sun isn't completely gone yet.

"Hi!" Jonah says, swimming over to me. "How cool is this? We can talk!"

I am afraid to open my mouth in case I swallow a gallon of water and drown. But I do it. I open my lips in a little circle and take a tiny breath in. I do not choke.

"It works!" I say, amazed. I have no idea *how* it works, but it is working. I am breathing and talking underwater. No scuba equipment necessary.

I thought I would sink to the bottom, but I'm not. I'm just floating. It's like I'm in one of those gravity-less spaceships and I can go up or down or anywhere I want.

We swim farther into the deep.

There are brightly colored fish swimming in all directions. A family of turtles meanders by us. And coral is everywhere. It looks like pipe cleaners gently blowing in the wind. Yellow, red, orange, blue, green. The water doesn't even feel cold anymore, just like a really nice bath.

Jonah is having the time of his life. He's laughing, somersaulting. He's even yodeling. Does he really have to let every sea creature know we're here?

"Can you try to be quiet?" I ask him, as a neon fish that's shaped like a trumpet smashes its nose against my knee. It does not seem to like me.

"Why? This is awesome."

"Jonah! This is serious business! You've been acting like a two-year-old since we got here!"

"You've been acting like a forty-year-old!" he snaps back. "This is supposed to be fun."

"No, it isn't!" I yell back as the trumpet fish goes after my big toe. "We're helping Lana."

"Why can't helping Lana be fun?"

"Because . . . because . . . You're impossible," I say, and turn my back on him. "Let's go to the sea witch and get this over with." We have to stay on schedule. We have to see the sea witch. But first we have to *find* the sea witch.

I pull the map up to my eyes. Unfortunately, the map has disintegrated in the water.

"Crumbs!" I yell.

Jonah turns back to me. "What's wrong?"

"Unlike us, the map was not waterproof."

He bites his lower lip. "I think I remember the way. Follow me."

"You think, or you *know*?"

He shrugs. "I think."

"Time is ticking, Jonah!"

"Well," he says, swimming forward, "then we'd better get kicking."

I nervously follow Jonah through seaweed, around coral, and over a cave. I feel bad for snapping at him, but honestly, he doesn't take anything seriously.

By now the water has started to get dark. Really dark. I press the light on my watch to illuminate our path and pray that the batteries don't die.

We swim for what feels like at least another hour.

I could really use a snack. That sushi potion was just not enough. I wish I'd had time to pack a picnic lunch from the wedding buffet. I'm going to miss that lemon meringue pie.

At the end of the cave, Jonah turns left and points.

"That's it," he says.

I shine my light up ahead. I have no doubt that he's right. If someone asked me to design a sea witch's house, this is what I'd create.

The walls are gray stone and covered in black sea-sludge. The path to the doorway is surrounded by barracudas and floating fish skeletons. There's a low moaning sound all around us. Jonah slows down and takes my hand.

"Maybe we should find a doorbell or something. The sea witch might not be the type of person who likes to be surprised." I see a big knocker in the shape of a human skull. With a trembling hand, I bang the knocker against the door.

Slowly the door creeps open.

"Come in," we hear. The voice is definitely female, but low and raspy.

We swim through the entranceway, terrified.

There she sits in the middle of the room. Well, not sits. Lies sideways on a black couch. She is not what I expected at all. She's beautiful. She's a mermaid just like Lana, but her tail is dark purple instead of green and orange. She's younger than I expected, too — she looks about my mom's age. She has black, waist-length hair.

Beside the couch is a large gray pot. No, it's not a pot. It's a cauldron. It's made of stone, and bubbles are steaming out of it. It looks like a hot tub — but a really, really scary one. I do not want to go anywhere near that cauldron if I can help it. I take a step back.

"Who are you?" the sea witch drawls. Her voice is smoky. It makes me want to move closer, but I resist.

"I'm-I'm-I'm Abby," I stutter. "And this is my brother, Jonah."

"Hello," she says. "I'm Nelly."

I nod. "We're here on behalf of Lana. I'm her —" I pause. "I'm her lawyer."

The sea witch cackles. "Her lawyer? Lana has a lawyer?"

I nod. "And I'm here to negotiate a deal."

"How are you even down here? Did you take the underwater potion?"

We nod.

Nelly laughs again. "Well, you'd better start negotiating before your time runs out."

"Right." I nervously clear my throat. It's been about two hours, which means we have ten hours left. We can convince her to help us in ten hours, can't we? "We would like you to reverse the spell you put on Lana," I say, my voice trembling.

She raises a perfectly arched eyebrow. "Which one?"

I half smile. "All of them?"

"Let's see," Nelly says. "There's the spell that changed her tail into legs. There's the spell that took away her voice. Then there's the spell that says that if the prince marries anyone else, she'll die before the next sunrise, which is at six oh five A.M."

"All of them would be good," I say. "But the dying one is definitely our priority."

"Reversing spells isn't cheap. What will you give me?"

I clear my throat. "What do you want?" Oops. This may have been a tiny oversight on my part. I came to negotiate with the sea witch but I didn't bring anything to trade. Never mind being a failed maid of honor — I'm a failed lawyer, too.

Nelly eyes Jonah. "The boy?"

Jonah scoots into my side.

"Um, no." Even though we're kind of in a fight, she still can't have my brother. "Is there anything else you want?"

She looks me over. "What is that on your wrist?"

I look down. "You want my watch? I can give you my watch." Not that I really want to give away my watch, but of course I'll do it to save Lana's *life*. I'm not sure how we'll find our way back to the shore without any light, though. I guess I'll worry about that problem later.

The sea witch nods. "Here's my offer. You give me the watch."

"Okay," I say. Maybe this won't be so hard after all.

"And in return for the watch, I'll give you a knife. You'll use the knife to stab the prince in the heart. Then I'll undo all the spells. Lana can go back to her life as a mermaid."

Is she kidding me?

"Um, that's not going to work, either," I say. "I am not going to kill someone." Sure, the prince is a bit of a jerk, but that doesn't mean I want him dead. And that definitely doesn't mean that I would ever consider killing him. I want to *be* a lawyer, not *need* a lawyer. "Can't I just give you the watch, and you'll reverse the spells?"

She snorts. "Reverse all the spells for one measly watch? No. One of you stabs the prince, or nothing. You know what? I don't even want a watch. The girl and I had a deal. She's the one who wasn't satisfied with her life even though she had *everything*. She had family who loved her! She was a princess! She was beautiful! But no, no, no, she wanted to give it all up to be *human*. She's a jerk! Just like her father!"

"But she wasn't happy!" I say. "She risked everything for a different life. She's not a jerk. She's . . . she's . . . brave! And you're a coward. You just hide in your cave and steal from people. You want everyone to be as miserable as you are."

Nelly blinks. And then blinks again. "Unless you have something better than a watch to trade, then we're done here."

Now what are we supposed to do? Wait. "Why is Lana's dad a jerk?" I wonder.

She ignores my question and instead says, "I guess we're done. Samuel! My dear Samuel! Show these children the door!"

My dear Samuel? "Don't tell me she has a boyfriend," I say.

But no. Just then a shark — an actual shark — swims up to us with a menacing look on its face.

I'm not that surprised her only companion is a shark — no person could love someone that mean.

"We're getting out of here," I say, and pull Jonah straight out of the house.

By the time we reach the black water, my heart is beating about three thousand miles a minute.

"That didn't go well," Jonah says.

"No, it didn't," I say, leaning against something soft and squishy that I hope won't eat me. I try to catch my breath. "Now what?"

"I can think of one person who might help us," Jonah says.

"Who?"

"The Sea King."

I nod. "It's time to find Lana's dad."

* chapter nineteen *

Sticks and Stones

I remember that, in the movie, the king offers to trade places with the Little Mermaid," Jonah explains as we start swimming again. "Maybe he'll want to do that now."

My heart clenches. "So the king dies instead of Lana? We don't want that, either!"

"Hopefully he'll have a better idea than that," Jonah says. "But we have to find him and ask. Don't you think our parents would want to know if we were facing a life-or-death situation?"

"We face life-and-death situations every time we go into the mirror!" I say.

"True," Jonah says. "But still."

"Okay," I say. Maybe the king can force the witch to recant her spell. Or maybe he'll have something to trade. Clearly he knows the sea witch — she called him a jerk.

So we're going to talk to him. But first we have to find him. Which we can't seem to do. We swim and swim, but we keep passing the same cave.

We're lost. We're very, very lost.

And there's something really freaky about being lost underwater in the dark. Beige coral reef sways in the wind and looks like fingers trying to grab us. Silvery fish appear to have teeth.

I light up my watch. It says six thirty, which means it must be around midnight here. How much longer can we swim in circles?

"We know you," a voice says.

"Did you say something?" Jonah asks.

"No," I say. "I thought it was you." A chill creeps down my spine. "Hello?" I say timidly. "Is someone there?"

"Yes," another voice says.

"We are," says a third voice.

We're surrounded.

"Who are you?" I ask, and aim my watch light at the voices. The light reveals a mermaid. No — five mermaids. All with green-and-orange swishing tails. The tops they're wearing look familiar, but I can't figure out from where.

"We're Lana's sisters," the one in the middle says. She has short, butter-colored hair and she's wearing a white sweater. "We've been spying on her, but we can't get too close to the shore. Is Lana okay?"

"Not exactly," I say, before explaining the whole story.

"We have to go talk to my dad!" one sister wearing a purple hoodie cries. "He has to help."

"We were trying to find him," I say. "Isn't it the middle of the night? What were you guys doing?"

"We were at a party," another one says, giving the necklace she's wearing an anxious twirl. Her brown hair is tied back in a tight braid and she's wearing a light-green shirt with a collar. "It's past curfew, though — we're definitely going to get in trouble."

"It's worth it for Lana," the mermaid in the hoodie says. "Follow me!"

We follow her through a winding path, past schools of striped and speckled fish, sparkly red coral, and even a twenty-foot-long shipwreck that's jammed into a bunch of rocks.

Two of the sisters swim by me, both wearing what look a lot like pajama tops.

Familiar pajama tops.

I glance at all the sisters. Purple hoodie. Green shirt. White sweater. Wait a sec.

"Those are my clothes!" I exclaim. "You found my suitcase!"

They spin around. "That was yours?" the one in the hoodie asks.

"Yes!" I say. "I thought I lost it."

"You did lose it," the one with the braid mutters. "Finder's keepers." She looks like the youngest of the bunch.

"Sasha," the one with the short hair and white sweater scolds. "We'll give them back their stuff." She looks like the oldest.

"Can we keep the wood paddles and the ball?" the one in my hoodie asks. "We made up a whole game with them where we hit the ball back and forth."

"That's how you're supposed to play," Jonah says. "It's called Kadima."

"We love Kadima," she says.

"Me too!" Jonah says. "We should play if we have time."

"There's no time for Kadima!" the oldest sister and I both yell. We look at each other and smile.

Soon we get to what appears to be a town. It's pretty empty because it's the middle of the night, but there's one restaurant still open.

"Where are we?" I ask.

"That's Salties," one of the sisters tells me. "It's the nicest restaurant on the Main Canal."

A few mermaids and mermen are sitting outside, enjoying the night. Instead of being pitch-black, like I expected, there are little sparkling lights lining the canal.

"Where do the lights come from?" I ask the oldest sister.

"Bioluminescence," she says. "Underwater life that glows in the dark."

Everyone looks at us curiously as we swim past — we are the only ones without tails — but we don't stop to sightsee.

Finally we spot what has to be the castle.

It's just as nice, if not nicer, than Prince Mortimer's palace. It's made of stone and cliffs and covered in protective coral.

"Let's go straight to Dad's room," the oldest says. "Follow me!"

No need for stairs in this palace. We swim right up into the king's windowless room. Not much security here.

"Dad! Dad!" the oldest one cries, swimming over to his bed.

"What's wrong, girls?" the king asks, opening his eyes.

He has dark hair that's gray at the temples. He also has one of those chins with a cleft in it.

He spots us. "Why did you bring humans?"

"They're friends of Lana's. And Lana needs our help."

Quickly I spill out the whole story. ". . . So you see," I say once I've finished, "we didn't know who else to go to. Do you have anything the sea witch would want? Or could you command her to reverse the spell? Maybe threaten to put her in ocean prison?"

The king looks shocked, yet I notice a determined glint in his eye. "Poor Lana! We must save her at once. Girls! Collect all the family jewels. The necklaces! The rings! All of Mom's old stuff!"

"Not the jewelry!" one of the sisters cries. "It's all we have left of Mom!"

"Your mom would want us to use it." The king throws off his covers. "Everyone, follow me."

✳ chapter twenty ✳

We're Back

It's not the most inviting décor," I say as I push a floating fish skeleton out of the way and knock on the door. I glance at my watch. We have to move fast. We've been underwater for almost nine-and-a-half hours. We still need two hours to get back to the beach.

"Go away!" Nelly yells from inside. "Didn't I tell you to stop bothering me?"

The door swings open and the sea witch has a scowl on her face. But suddenly her expression changes. Softens. She blinks. And then blinks again. She's looking above my head and I turn to see that she's staring at the king.

And he's staring at her.

"What do *you* want?" she asks.

The king blushes.

"Nelly," I say, "the king is here to offer you jewelry. If you'll save his daughter."

"Right!" the king says, snapping out of his trance. "May we come in?"

Nelly tears her eyes away from the king and checks out our whole group. "All of you?"

"Yes," I say. I put my hands on my hips and clench them into fists, hoping I look defiant.

"I guess." Nelly sweeps her arm to the side in an exaggerated gesture of welcome, and all eight of us float-march in.

"I haven't seen you in years," the king says.

"No, you haven't," Nelly says, tight-lipped.

"How do you know each other?" I ask.

"We went to elementary school together," the king says.

"We certainly did," Nelly says, crossing her arms and slapping her tail against the ground. "How could I forget? You used to call me a horrible name."

The king's eyes widen in surprise. "What are you talking about? I called you Jelly Nelly!"

She scowls. "Exactly. Jelly Nelly. Because I reminded you of a jellyfish."

"So why is that horrible?" the king asks, his forehead wrinkling.

"Because jellyfish are annoying and poisonous," Nelly spits out.

I'd have to agree. Jellyfish are kind of the mosquitoes of the sea.

The king shakes his head. "Jellyfish are smart. And beautiful. And fascinating."

"They are not," Nelly says, but her voice wavers.

"They are so," he says. "I called you Jelly Nelly because I had a crush on you."

Nelly blushes. "You did?"

"You did?" we all echo.

Now it's the king's turn to blush.

Nelly makes a strange sound. Was it a giggle? She clears her throat. "Oh. I just assumed . . ." Her voice trails off. "I had no idea." She wraps a strand of her dark hair around her finger. She giggles again. Is Nelly flirting? Does the sea witch *like* the king?

"Well, now you know," he says. He's all flushed. "It's nice to see you again." Oh. My. Goodness. Does he still *like* the witch?

145

But then he shakes his head. "No. It's *not* nice. You have to help my daughter."

Nelly crosses her arms. "I don't have to do anything."

He straightens up, flirting forgotten. "We have jewels to offer you. In exchange for you changing the spell you put on Lana. Girls, show her what you have. Nelly, take whatever you want. But please, spare my daughter."

The oldest steps up and opens her hand to reveal a sparkling ring. "I have a diamond engagement ring."

The second oldest opens her hand next. "I have emerald earrings."

The third shows us a chunky bracelet. "It's fourteen-carat gold."

The fourth has two hoop earrings dangling on her thumb. "They're platinum."

Sasha, the youngest, steps up and points to her neck. "I'm wearing a mother-of-pearl necklace. I guess you can have it."

Hold on a minute. "That's my necklace!" I exclaim.

Sasha shrugs. "Don't you want to help Lana?"

I sigh. "You can have it," I tell Nelly.

Nelly eyes the goods. "Hmm," she says. "They're pretty, but I already have my own jewelry." She wiggles her fingers in front of us, and we see that they are glittering with jewels. "Do you have anything else?"

"Um . . ." We look at each other. We are empty-handed. We are out of stuff.

"You can have my Kadima paddles," Jonah offers.

"What's Kadima?" Nelly asks, intrigued.

"It's a game," Jonah says. "You and another person hit a ball back and forth. It's very fun."

Nelly's face clouds over. "I don't want a game," she snarls. "Who am I going to play it with? Samuel doesn't have hands. If you have nothing else to offer, I think we're done here."

A lightbulb goes off in my head. She doesn't want Kadima *paddles*. She wants someone to play Kadima *with*.

Before I thought no one could love her because she was mean. But maybe she's so mean because no one loves her.

I know how to save Lana.

"Would you consider reversing the spells on Lana in exchange for a date?" I blurt out.

Nelly blinks. "Excuse me?"

"A date," I repeat. My mouth feels dry. This has to work. It just has to.

147

Nelly blushes and looks down at the sandy floor. "A date with whom?"

I glance at the king. His cheeks are just as red as Nelly's. He's just as lonely as Nelly.

He swims forward. "With me," he says.

Their eyes meet across the room.

"Really?" she asks softly.

He nods. He takes another step toward her. "Would you like to go out sometime, Jelly Nelly? Or I can just call you Nelly."

"Just Nelly is good," she says. And then giggles.

Yes! This is going to work! Way to go, me! Speaking of going — we have to get a move on.

"So do we have a deal?" I ask. "A date in exchange for reversing the spells? You can go to Salties!"

"What if she hurts our dad?" the youngest mermaid cries. "She's a witch, and he's all we have left!"

Good point.

"Can you give us some sort of collateral?" the oldest mermaid asks, running her fingers through her short hair.

Nelly nods toward the shark. "You can keep Samuel as a pet until the date is done. He needs a babysitter, anyway. He eats the couch when he's lonely."

Better the couch than me.

"So," I ask again. "Do we have a deal?"

We all hold our breath.

Nelly and the king nod. "Deal," they say simultaneously, and then they both laugh and turn red again.

"Let's shake on it," the king says, putting out his hand.

"Abby," Jonah says, tugging at my sleeve.

"One sec, Jonah," I say, wanting to see how this ends.

Nelly takes his outstretched hand.

We wait for them to shake, but instead, they both just stand there, holding each other's hands. And holding.

Still holding.

All righty, then.

"Abby," Jonah says again. "I don't feel so good. My chest feels heavy."

I glance at my watch. The potion is going to run out in two hours! We have to go.

"Abby," Jonah says again, and crumples into a heap on the sandy ground.

I lunge after him. But before I can reach him, the room starts to spin. I feel intense pressure on my chest. Like someone's sitting on me. Or like I'm underwater and I can't breathe.

Oh, no.

The potion ran out early.

"Jonah!" I try to yell — but nothing comes out. The people around me look murkier and murkier until I don't see anything at all.

* chapter twenty-one *

Ashore

abby, Abby. You have to get up."

The next thing I see is light. A very bright light.

I open my eyes. Where am I? What happened?

I sit up, cough, and notice Lana kneeling beside me.

"Finally," she says, her eyes squinting in concern. "How do you feel?"

The last thing I remember, we were underwater. And now it's just me and Lana on the beach. I'm so confused. "How did I get here?"

"My family brought you up, and then I pulled you onto the beach."

I'm still a bit dizzy and disoriented.

Wait a sec. I'm on the beach. Jonah's not. Oh, no. Oh no, oh no, oh no. "Where's my brother?"

She hesitates. "He's, um . . ."

My heart stops. He drowned. He drowned, and it's all my fault. Plus I was so mean to him today. I was awful. He was just being his totally awesome fun self, and I yelled at him. I try to breathe, but I can't.

". . . There he is," she says.

What? He's alive? I jump to my feet and spot him hopping his way down the beach.

"Jonah!" I shriek. "You're alive!" I throw my arms around his neck.

"Of course I'm alive," he says. "I was just getting myself a snack. I'm starving." He's munching on French fries and mustard. "Glad you're finally awake."

I let go of his neck even though I don't want to. "How long was I out for?"

"A few hours."

"What happened?"

"Either we didn't take enough potion each, or the recipe wasn't exactly right."

I hug him hard. "I'm so sorry I was mean to you."

"I'm sorry I made you do all the work," he says. "Want a fry? The mustard isn't as awful as you'd think."

"Sure," I say.

"Me too," Lana says.

"What time is it?" I wonder.

"Almost ten A.M."

I look at Lana in surprise. "It's ten o'clock, and you're still alive!"

She nods. "I am."

"And you can talk!"

She nods again. "Nelly reversed the spell. And gave me back my voice."

"That's amazing!" I cheer. "We did it! We fixed the story! Everything is back the way it was!"

"Not everything," Jonah says.

"What do you mean?" I ask, munching on another fry. Jonah's right. The mustard isn't that bad.

He motions to Lana. "She still has legs."

He's right. She *does* still have legs. "What happened? Nelly wouldn't let you have your tail back? She's making you stay on land forever? I thought we had done so well! Did your dad cancel the date or something?"

Lana shakes her head. "No, that's not it. She offered to give me my tail back, but I told her I didn't want it."

Huh? "Why not?"

"I love my family, but I don't want to leave the surface. Prince or not, it's my home. I love to walk and dance. And I really love sunsets. And shoops — I mean, shoes. And books. And paintings. And have you tried a cheeseburger with mustard and that yellow-y American cheese? They're amazing."

I nod.

She goes on. " And even though I have my voice back, I have another voice now that I'm not ready to give up."

I don't understand what she's talking about. "You have a second voice?"

"Yes! Thanks to you, I can write! And that's given me a whole new voice. I want to stay on land and write stories about the world under the ocean. I want to write books about mermaids and share them with humans so they don't think merfolk are make-believe!"

"I would love to read those," I say. "Is your dad okay with you staying?"

She nods. "He said he was going to miss me, but he also gave me these." She opens her hand, and I see the diamond ring, the emerald earrings, and the bracelet. "They belonged to my mother. He told me I can sell them and buy a house with a big dock so he and my sisters can always visit."

"That's amazing," I say, throwing my arms around Lana in a hug. "Everything worked out."

"Almost," Jonah says. "We still have to get home."

Oh, no! If it's almost ten here, we only have two hours to get back, and we still have no idea how. "What are we going to do?" I ask.

"It's all taken care of," Jonah says smugly. "By me."

"But, Jonah, we're sitting on the beach. Not in our basement."

"Not for long," Jonah says, and then he points to the water.

In the distance, I see the five mermaid sisters, plus Nelly, plus the king.

"She's finally awake!" the oldest mermaid says.

"Hi, guys!" Lana yells. She splashes out into the water and hugs them all. Aw. We got them back together.

"Carolyn made us more underwater potion," Jonah says. "She made double, just to be safe."

"How does that help?" I ask. "We don't live underwater."

"Nelly's cauldron is underwater. It's going to take us home."

"But Nelly isn't a fairy," I say. "Is she?"

He shrugs. "She said she could do it."

"She did? Did you have to trade her something?"

He shook his head. "She said it's payment for reintroducing her to the king."

"Oh!" If being a judge doesn't work out, maybe I can be a matchmaker. "When do we go?"

"Now!"

I look back up at the palace. "Should we say good-bye?"

"I said good-bye for both of us. Carolyn said she'll miss us. And she promised to teach Lana how to cook."

"Don't worry," Lana says. "I promise not to make shark."

"And Vivian packed up all our stuff and put them in your suitcase."

"Whose suitcase?"

"Your suitcase! The mermaids gave it back."

"Oh! Great! What about the stuff inside the suitcase?"

"They gave that back, too. Lana put your necklace around your neck when you were sleeping. I tried to do it myself, but that clasp is really confusing."

I reach up and feel my necklace. "Thanks, Jonah. Thanks, Lana."

"No problem," Lana says.

"I gave Lana's sisters my Kadima paddles," Jonah says. "They seemed to really like them."

"That was sweet of you, Jonah." I turn to Lana.

Lana takes the cup of potion, spits in it, and then hands it to me. "I'm going to miss you two. Thank you for everything."

I chug the still-disgusting potion, and then give Lana a tight hug. "Your stories are going to be amazing."

"Thanks. I can't wait to write them."

Jonah gives her a hug, too.

"I'll see you tomorrow, everyone!" she calls to her family. "Have fun on your date, Dad! But don't make any trades, okay? And I'll miss you, Abby and Jonah!"

We wave. Here we go. With one hand, I hold on to my brother, and with the other, I hold on to my suitcase. Just like when I came, but now with extra yellow clothes. I dunk right away.

Sometimes you just gotta go for it.

This time when we go underwater, the ocean is alive with activity. Mermaids and mermen everywhere. Everyone's busy, swimming this way or that. It's like we were dropped in the busiest aquarium in the world.

I wish we had more time to explore. Maybe we'll come back one day?

When we arrive at Nelly's house, everything looks different. Maybe because it's bright outside. Or maybe because she did some spring cleaning of the skeletons and stuff.

"Thank you," Nelly whispers to me.

I try not to stiffen as she gives me a hug.

"Because we reintroduced you to the king?" I ask.

"Yes. And because you were right. Instead of changing my own life, I wanted everyone to be as miserable as I was. I *was* a coward."

We hug all the sisters, and then we are ready to go. "What do we do?" I ask, eyeing the bubbling cauldron with a little bit of fear.

"Just swim right into it," Nelly says.

"We won't burn?"

"You shouldn't."

"But I don't understand," I say. "I thought only fairies could get us home."

"I *am* a fairy," she says.

Huh? "We thought you were a witch," Jonah says.

"A witch is a fairy who does bad things," she says. "See, it depends what you use your magic for."

Aha. That makes sense. I look toward the cauldron. "We can't both fit in," I say. Not together.

"I'll go first," Jonah says.

"I'm not letting you go alone!" I say.

"Then hold on to my foot."

"Okay," I say. I grab hold of his very wet sneaker with one hand and the suitcase with the other. "Ready?" I ask.

"Ready!" he says. "Hold on tight!"

He swims, swims, swims right toward the cauldron. It squeezes but doesn't hurt. I close my eyes and trust Jonah to get us home.

✳ chapter twenty-two ✳

Dry, Again

the next thing I know, I'm in a very large puddle on my basement floor, still holding Jonah's foot. We've slid across half the floor like we're at a water park.

"Well done," I hear.

"You too," Jonah and I both say at the same time.

"That wasn't me," I say. My spine tingles. "That wasn't you?" He shakes his head.

"But, Jonah, if it wasn't me, and it wasn't you . . ." I look back at the mirror. It's still swirling. "Maryrose? Was that you?"

She doesn't answer. But that had to have been her! It must

have been! She talked to us! She finally talked to us! And she said "well done"!

What does "well done" mean? "Was changing the tale what we were supposed to do?" I ask the mirror. "Do you have a plan for us?"

She still doesn't answer.

"Abby, what time is it?" Jonah asks.

I look at my watch. "It's four minutes to seven."

"We gotta go!"

He's right. Our parents will be waking us up any minute. I turn back to the mirror. "I have a lot of questions for you," I say. "And next time, I would really appreciate it if you could answer them." I leave the wet suitcase downstairs because it's filled with water and ridiculously heavy. I cross my fingers and hope I have a chance to deal with it before my parents find it.

We dash up the stairs. When we're on the main floor, I hear the ringing of my parents' alarm clock. "Run! Run!" I whisper to Jonah. "Go put on your pj's, hide your wet clothes in the back of your closet, and get into bed! Love you! I'm glad you didn't drown!"

"Love you, too!" Jonah says as he sprints toward his bedroom. "I'm glad you didn't drown, either!"

Our doors close just as I hear my parents' door opening. Oh no, oh no, oh no! I rip off my clothes, look for a clean pair of pajamas, remember I don't have any, jump under my covers, and pull them up to my neck as my doorknob starts to wiggle.

About half a second later, my door creeps open. "Morning, honey," my mom says. "Time to get up."

I fake a yawn. "Thanks, Mom!"

I hear a bang from Jonah's room. Mom looks quizzically in his direction. Oh, no! He's not ready yet. I need to distract her! What do I do?

"Wait! Mom?"

She leans against the doorway. "Yes, honey?"

"I want to talk to you about something."

"Yes?" she asks expectantly.

At first I have no idea what I want to say, but then, suddenly, I do.

I spot my jewelry box on my dresser and think about Lana. I had wanted her to accept her life as is, but she wanted to fight for her dreams. Sure, sometimes you have to get what you get and not get upset. But maybe other times, you have to follow your heart and go after what you really want. Take a risk. Be brave.

I guess part of growing up is learning when to do which.

"Mom," I start. "I know you're really busy. I understand. But I think I'm old enough to go to Chicago by myself. There's a program where they let kids fly by themselves — they call them UMs. Undercover Minors? No, Unidentified Minors. No —"

"Unaccompanied Minors!" Jonah screams out from his room.

"Thanks!" I yell back. "Jonah told me that his friend Isaac takes airplanes by himself to visit his dad, and he's only seven. Can I do that to visit Nana?"

"Oh, honey! By yourself? Are you sure you're up for that?"

I nod. If I can navigate the deepest part of the ocean, I can definitely get around the airport. I don't say that part to my mom.

"You wouldn't find it scary?"

"I might," I say. "But being a little scared is worth it to see Nana."

Mom sighs. "I'll tell you what — I don't know much about this UM program, but it sounds like a possibility. I'll look into it, okay?"

"Thanks, Mom. I can do it, I swear."

"I have no doubt that you can," she says softly. She inhales deeply. "You smell delicious. Like the beach."

I laugh. I can't help it.

She looks at me quizzically. "Do you have a suntan?"

"Er, no," I say. "It's just the light."

She nods and tousles my hair. "Maybe when all this work is done, we should go to Florida for a week off."

"Sounds good to me," I say. She may wonder where we got our new swimsuits.

"Hey, honey, why aren't you wearing any pajamas?"

"Oh . . . um . . ." I think back to the story of *The Emperor's New Clothes*. If I tell my mom I'm actually wearing pj's will she pretend to believe me? Probably not. "They're too tight," I say, suddenly inspired. "I need new ones. I'm a growing girl, you know."

"Oh, I know," she says, and smiles. "I'll have to take you shopping. Now go get dressed and then come down for breakfast, 'kay? Time for school."

I nod. Even though I'm tired, I'm excited to see Frankie and Robin. I wish I could tell them what I've been up to, but I don't think we're supposed to tell anyone.

Hmm. Are we not supposed to tell anyone, or just not our parents?

Could I bring Frankie and Robin with us next time? Would the mirror let them in?

Once my mom leaves, I jump out of bed and pick up my jewelry box.

Lana is no longer a mermaid. Instead, she has legs. She's lying on her stomach, propped up by her elbows, wearing a yellow sundress and strappy sandals. She's writing in a notebook.

She's a real writer! Yay!

I wonder if she found a worthy prince. Or maybe a worthy surfer. I wonder if I'll ever see her again. I wonder where the mirror will take me next.

I study the other characters on my jewelry box. I've always wanted to meet Sleeping Beauty. And Rapunzel. And that flying carpet really does look like fun. I'll just have to hold on extra tight.

I'm ready, Maryrose. For answers. For excitement. For our next adventure. Wherever it may be.

DON'T MISS ABBY AND JONAH'S NEXT ADVENTURE!

Whatever After #4
DREAM ON

This time, Abby and Jonah get pulled into the story of Sleeping Beauty — along with Abby's friend Robin! Even worse, Robin pricks her finger on the spindle, leaving Sleeping Beauty wide awake. Will they be able to fix this nightmare?

acknowledgments

Thank you to my awesome agents, publishers, first readers, and friends: Laura Dail, Tamar Rydzinski, Brian Lipson, Aimee Friedman, Abby McAden, David Levithan, Becky Shapiro, Becky Amsel, Bess Braswell, Allison Singer, Janet Robbins, Elizabeth Parisi, Lizette Serrano, Emily Heddleson, Candace Greene, AnnMarie Anderson, Courtney Sheinmel, Emily Bender, Anne Heltzel, Lauren Myracle, E. Lockhart, Tori, Carly and Carol Adams, Avery and Whitney Carmichael, Targia Clarke, Jess Braun, Lauren Kisilevsky, Bonnie Altro, Susan Finkelberg-Sohmer, Corinne and Michael Bilerman, Debbie Korb, Joanna Steinberg, Casey Klurfeld, Jess Rothenberg, Adele Griffin, Leslie Margolis, Robin Wasserman, Maryrose Wood, Tara Altebrando, Sara Zarr, Ally Carter, Jennifer Barnes, Alan Gratz, Penny Fransblow, Maggie Marr, and Farrin Jacobs.

Love and thanks to my family: Aviva, Mom, Robert, Dad, Louisa, Gary, Lori, Sloane, Isaac, Vickie, John, Gary, Darren, Ryan, Jack, Jen, Teri, Briana, Michael, David, Patsy, Murray, Maggie, and Jenny. Extra love and extra thanks and lots and lots of kisses to Chloe, Anabelle, and Todd.

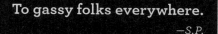

To gassy folks everywhere.

—S.P.

Fart Squad

Text copyright © 2015 by Full Fathom Five, LLC
Illustrations copyright © 2015 by Full Fathom Five, LLC

All rights reserved. Printed in the United States of America. No part of this book may be used or repro-
duced in any manner whatsoever without written permission except in the case of brief quotations
embodied in critical articles and reviews. For information address HarperCollins Children's Books, a
division of HarperCollins Publishers, 195 Broadway, New York, NY 10007.
www.harpercollinschildrens.com

Library of Congress Cataloging-in-Publication Data
Pilger, Seamus.
   Fart Squad / by Seamus Pilger. — First edition.
      pages cm — (Fart squad ; 1)
   Summary: After their lunches are stolen, Harry Buttz Elementary School students Darren, Tina,
Juan-Carlos, and Walter eat radioactive burritos that give each a strange ability—along with serious
gas—which, with training by Janitor Stan, may help them foil Number Two and the BO twins' evil plan.
   ISBN 978-0-06-236631-3 (hardback) — ISBN 978-0-06-229045-8 (pbk.)
   [1. Flatulence—Fiction. 2. Ability—Fiction. 3. Middle schools—Fiction. 4. Schools—Fiction. 5. Janitors—
Fiction. 6. Humorous stories.] I. Title.
PZ7.1.P55Far 2015
[Fic]—dc23   2014027412
                                                                                                           CIP
                                                                                                            AC

Design by Victor Joseph Ochoa
15 16 17 18 19   CG/OPM   10 9 8 7 6 5 4 3 2
❖
First Edition

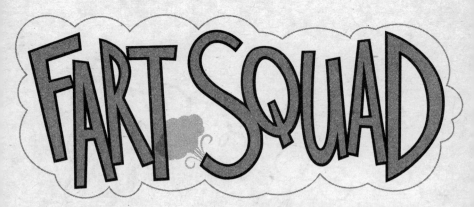

FART SQUAD

by **SEAMUS PILGER**

illustrated by **STEPHEN GILPIN**

HARPER

An Imprint of HarperCollinsPublishers

CHAPTER ONE

Darren Stonkadopolis was determined to make it to the end of the school year without getting into any more trouble.

He was the kind of kid who was always running when he should be walking, squirming when he should be sitting, and talking sports when he should be listening in math. His hair was always a mess and his jeans almost instantly wore out. People thought he had a twin because he often seemed to be in two places at once. His mom liked to say that he had "energy to burn," while his teachers thought he was trouble. He seemed to spend as much time in the principal's office as in class, and every time Miss Priscilly sent him to see Principal Dingleberry, it brought him closer to spending the summer at Harry Buttz Elementary School's "special" summer program, which would mean missing out on sports camp with his best friend, Andy.

So Darren was really trying his best to behave. Even though his stomach was growling. He hadn't eaten since breakfast—and that was almost three hours ago. . . .

"Slow down!" Andy called out as they dashed down the stairs

ahead of their class. A thick pair of glasses bounced atop his nose. He was smaller and skinnier than Darren even though he was only two days younger than his best friend. "Your lunch isn't going any-where!"

"Except my stomach!" Darren said. He'd worked up an appetite in gym class and couldn't wait to get back to their classroom, where their lunches were stashed on a shelf in the coat closet. "I'm starving. Stuck-in-the-desert, eat-your-own-leg starving!"

Darren expected that he and Andy would be the first ones back to the classroom, so he was sur-prised to find two kids, Bertha and Oscar Scroggy, rummaging around in the coat closet—where they didn't belong.

Bertha and Oscar were brother and sister. Everyone called them B.O.—in part because they were inseparable and in part because they were allergic to bathing. Darren recognized their smell before he even saw their faces.

"Hey!" he challenged them. "What are you doing here?"

The twins wheeled about as though surprised by the interruption. "None of your business, squirt," Bertha said with her mouth full. "Get lost."

"Yeah," Oscar snarled. "What she said."

The twins were the biggest bullies in school, in more ways than one. They had been held back so many times they were practically teenagers, and they weren't above using their size advantage to terrorize everybody else. Most kids tried to stay out of their way.

But Darren didn't back down. "This is our classroom, not yours."

Andy looked at Darren like he was crazy, but stood by his friend. "Um, maybe you took a wrong turn?"

"Oh, yeah?" Bertha said, ignoring Andy. She and Oscar stomped toward the boys, clenching their fists. "You got a problem with that?"

Darren realized he might have rushed into things a little too fast . . . again. He felt bad about dragging Andy into this mess as well. One of these days he really needed to learn to control himself. . . .

He braced for some serious wedgy action—or worse—but was saved by the sound of the rest of their class catching up to them.

Bertha and Oscar scowled at the interruption. "Ah, this place is for babies anyway," Bertha muttered. She shoved her way past Darren and Andy and headed out into the hall. "C'mon, bro. We've got better places to be."

Oscar followed her out the door. "Later, losers."

Andy let out a sigh of relief. "Whew, that was a close one. What do you think they were doing here in the first place?"

"Nothing good," Darren guessed, but he was too hungry to worry about that now. His stomach was growling so loudly he could barely hear his own thoughts. He hurried over to the coatroom—but all that was there for him was a horrible discovery. "My lunch! It's missing!"

· "Are you sure?" Andy helped him search the closet, even as the other kids arrived to claim their own lunch boxes and bag lunches. "Maybe you just misplaced it?"

"No!" Darren insisted. "I put it in the same place every day, right here on the shelf. You know I don't fool around when it comes to my lunch, especially on a day like today—pickles-and-sauerkraut sandwich—my favorite."

"The B.O. twins must have swiped it," Andy guessed. "Bertha had her mouth full, after all, and Oscar's pockets were bulging."

"I wouldn't put it past them," Darren said, but he was too hungry to worry about that now. "Must . . . have . . . food," he grunted. His legs felt like overcooked spaghetti, and his brain was foggy. "Get me to the cafeteria."

The hike to the cafeteria felt a zillion miles long. By the time they got there, most of their friends were already eating. Darren scrounged up some leftovers: an apple slice that was already turning brown, a pizza crust with teeth marks around the edge, and crumbs from the bottom of a crumpled bag of potato chips.

It wasn't enough. His body needed to refuel, and there was only one thing left to do.

"I'm gonna have to buy lunch."

Horrified gasps erupted around the table.

"You can't be serious!" Andy said. "Everybody knows that cafeteria food is roadkill."

"But I'm starving!" Darren insisted as he licked the last crumbs out of the bag of chips. "I've got no choice."

"Don't do it, man!" Andy pleaded. "Zero food is better than lunch-lady food!"

"I don't have a choice!" Darren said. He picked

up a tray and headed for the counter. "Wish me luck. I'm going in!"

Andy shook his head. "He's a dead man."

"Who? Darren?" Bootsie Brown arrived on the scene, sticking her nose in. Bootsie was the biggest snoop in school. She could smell another kid in trouble from two classrooms away. Her eyes zeroed in on Darren. "Okay, this I have to see!"

His friend's warnings rang in his ears as Darren got in the lunch line. To his horror, by the time he got his tray, all that was left was the infamous Five-Bean Burritos, the most dreaded of all the school lunches. A few of the specials, like the spaghetti or meat loaf, were at least semi-edible, but nobody in their right mind ever ate the burritos. Terrifying tales were told of what had happened to the last poor soul who had eaten them.

He eyed the burritos nervously. They looked as greasy and unappetizing as ever. Maybe even a little more so. But what could he do? Darren had run out of options. The horror stories had to just be rumors. How bad could they really be?

He piled a stack of greasy burritos onto his tray and carried them back to the table. A crowd of kids, including the B.O. twins, gathered around to watch.

"Bet you some nerd's lunch money that he throws up," Bertha said.

"You're on, sis," Oscar said, chortling. His breath smelled suspiciously of pickles and sauerkraut, but Darren had more immediate concerns at the moment.

More kids joined the bet. The smart money was on some serious puking . . . or worse.

"You know, the last kid who ate those had the runs for a month," Bootsie said. "It's true. I heard it from my cousin, who heard about it from a kid who knew a kid who used to go to this school. . . ."

"Nah," Andy insisted. "I heard that a kid barfed so much that they had to bring in fire hoses to clean up the cafeteria afterward!"

Darren turned and gave the B.O. twins a dirty look. If anything like that went wrong, he'd have them to blame.

"Here goes nothing," he said.

The crowd gasped in amazement as he wolfed down the burritos in record time. They were crunchier than he had expected, with an odd flavor he couldn't place. So he doused them with Tabasco sauce and cleaned off his whole plate. There was absolutely no puking involved. Lunch money exchanged hands.

"I don't believe it," Bootsie said.

"Me either," Andy said. "You must have been *really* hungry!"

Darren spotted a few other worried-looking kids daring to eat today's "special." He wondered if their lunches had gone missing, too. He was gobbling down the last burrito when the bell rang. He patted his stomach, feeling full at last.

But then on the way back to his homeroom, he felt an uncomfortable pressure start to build. By the time he was back at his desk, an embarrassing eruption seemed inevitable. Half-digested burritos churned angrily, filling his gut with toxic gas. He clenched his butt to hold it in, but the pressure kept building.

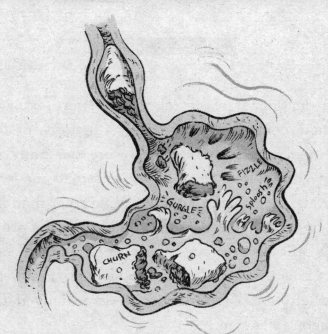

This was bad. Darren squirmed uncomfortably, hoping nobody would notice.

Fat chance.

"What's wrong with you?" Bootsie asked, loud enough for everyone to hear. Her hand shot up. "Miss Priscilly, Miss Priscilly, I think something's wrong with Dar—"

Darren gave her the evil eye.

The teacher, Miss Priscilly, glanced at him. "Are you all right, Darren?"

Miss Priscilly wasn't bad as teachers went, but she had one notable pet peeve. The young ladies and gentlemen of her classroom were expected to take control of their bodily functions or face the consequences. Mistakes were generally not allowed. Not long ago, a fellow classmate made the mistake of sneezing into his palm rather than into the crook of his elbow and wound up in the principal's office every recess for a week. Darren could only imagine where a burrito blooper from below the belt would land someone—especially if that someone was him.

"Uh-huh," he fibbed, barely able to sit still. He was clenching hard enough to turn coal into diamonds, but the volcanic eruption kept building inside him. His bloated stomach felt like it was about to burst. A chewed-up mess of burritos, Tabasco sauce, and soda boiled and bubbled in his belly. He knew he

SPLOOSH RUMBLE GURGLE

CLENCH

couldn't hold the fart in much longer.

Bootsie watched him like a hawk. Her nose twitched, anticipating trouble.

Darren had to think quickly or he was a goner. He was way past the point of asking for a bathroom pass. There was no telling what could happen on the long walk from his desk to the classroom door. Then he had an idea.

Why not try to redirect the fart? Burps were rude, too, but probably not as smelly and embarrassing as a fart. He placed a hand over his mouth and tried to swallow backward.

But the burp came out louder than he expected. Heads turned in his direction.

"Miss Priscilly!" Bootsie piped up again.

That was hardly necessary.

"Darren!" the offended teacher said. "Kindly control yourself."

"I'm trying," he insisted, "but—"

A few desks away, Andy groaned and buried his face in his hands.

"Try harder," Miss Priscilly said sternly.

But the pressure was already building up inside Darren again—and heading down below this time. Before Darren could even try to burp again, he let loose with a fart that caught the entire classroom by surprise.

To be clear, this wasn't just any fart. This was the Fart to End All Farts. A *blatt* so rude the map of the world crashed to the floor. The explosive force

of the fart knocked Darren right out of his chair and landed him on the floor at the front of the class.

The fart was loud and gross. A sulfurous stink, strong enough to make your eyes water, filled the whole classroom. Students gagged and covered their mouths and noses. Others tried to hold their breaths. Bootsie pinched her nose shut and looked at Darren in complete disgust. Darren scrambled back to his seat—and found it hot to the touch. His eyes bulged as he saw that the plastic seat had *melted.* And Miss Priscilly was so furious her face turned ten shades of crimson.

"Oooooooooooooooooout!" she ordered.

"But—" He tried to explain that it wasn't his fault, really. "The burritos—"

"Mr. Stonkadopolis, what you eat is your business, as long as I don't have to see it, smell it, or think about it. But now you've made it my business, and the principal's business as well."

"I swear, it wasn't on purpose . . . !"

"Fine. Then go see the nurse . . . and don't come back without a note confirming that your digestive difficulties are under control," she said. "Quickly. Before you go off again!"

Darren hurried out of the classroom, his butt burning. So much for staying out of trouble!

And the worst part was, he felt an even bigger fart coming on. . . .

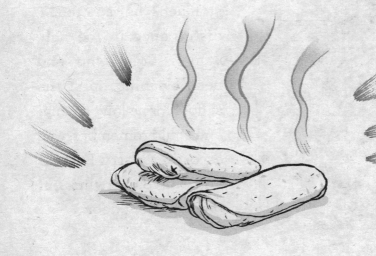

CHAPTER TWO

"I've told you before," the janitor said, "stay out of the basement."

As Darren trudged toward the nurse's office,  clutching his bloated stomach, he spotted a disturbance in the hall. Janitor Stan, who had been cleaning up at the school for as long as any-one could remember, was escorting Harry Buttz II and the B.O. twins out the basement door.

"You can't talk to me like that," Harry protested. "Don't you know who I am?"

Harry was the grandson of the school's namesake, a wealthy factory owner whose family had founded Buttzville generations ago. He had an expensive haircut, designer clothes, and, as usual, a hand down the back of his pants, furiously scratching at an itch that never seemed to go away, no matter what he tried. Despite his family name and all the campaign goodies he'd given away, he'd lost the last student body election because nobody would shake his hand.

"You tell him, Number Two!" Bertha said. She and Oscar hung out with Harry, mostly because he was rich and had all the newest computer games.

"Don't call me that!" Harry barked.

"Look, you three," Stan said. "I don't care what a big cheese Harry's dad is. The basement is off-limits.

Don't let me catch you snooping around there again."

"This is all your fault," Harry muttered to B.O. as the scratchy, smelly trio slunk away. "If you two could just follow simple directions . . ."

"Don't blame us," Bertha protested. "It's not our fault we were interrupted by a couple of nosy brats."

She glanced back over her shoulder, giving Darren the evil eye. Her hulking twin did likewise.

First the lunches, now this, Darren thought. *Those three are certainly keeping busy today.*

But before he could follow that thought through, he let another one rip. A thunderous fart echoed down the hall and polluted the air. There was no way Stan could miss it.

"Whoa!" the janitor exclaimed. "What was that?"

"Just some bad burritos," Darren explained.

"The lunchroom special?" Stan guessed. "Let me guess, Miss Priscilly sent you to the nurse's office, right?"

Nothing got past the eagle-eyed janitor, who always knew more about what was happening at the school than the principal and teachers. He knew which kids were friends, why certain kids weren't speaking to one another, what had become of any "misplaced" school supplies, and who exactly had toilet-papered the principal's car that one time. He had also covered for Darren in the past, like when all the biology class frogs had somehow gotten loose. (It was an accident. Really!)

"Something like that," Darren admitted. He tried to change the subject. "What was all that with Number Two and his goon squad?"

"No big deal," Stan said. "Just caught them poking around where they didn't belong . . . again. But don't let me slow you down. Run along now," he said, batting away the contaminated air in front of him. "Go see what the nurse can do for that unruly gut of yours."

Darren knew the way to the infirmary by heart, thanks to the many scrapes and sprains he had picked up playing too hard. When he got there, he found Nurse Rancid occupied with another patient: a tiny dark-haired girl in a pretty pink dress. She looked like a little princess. All that was missing was the tiara.

"Excuse me," he said. "Miss Priscilly sent me...."

"Just take a seat," the nurse replied. "I'll be with you in a sec."

But before Darren sat down, a foul smell filled the office. It was strong enough to make Darren hold his nose, but the effect on Nurse Rancid was even more impressive. "Oh my!" she gasped before collapsing onto the floor. She was out cold. This was not good. Darren needed a note from her if he wanted to get back to class, but as long as Nurse Rancid was passed out she wasn't going to be doing any writing of any kind.

Yikes, Darren thought. *Did I do that?*

He was pretty sure he hadn't farted this time, which left only one other suspect.

"Did *you* do that?" he asked the girl.

"Do what?" she asked innocently.

Darren furiously fanned Nurse Rancid in the hopes of reviving her. "You know...," he said. "Fart."

"Did you hear a fart?" she asked.

"No," he admitted.

"Then I must not have," she said.

"Or maybe your farts are just silent but deadly."

Just then, Nurse Rancid stirred. Darren ran to her desk to get a pen and notepad before she passed out again. Sure the nurse hadn't yet examined him, but maybe she'd be out of it enough not to realize. Because all he really needed to satisfy Miss Priscilly was a signed note.

But as soon as the nurse opened her eyes, an awful, pungent smell flooded the room and knocked her out cold again.

This time Darren *knew* he wasn't responsible. It had to be the girl again.

"Knock that off!" he said sharply.

"Knock what off?" she replied.

"You know what I mean!"

To be fair, holding a fart in was easier said than done. Before Darren could say another word, he lost control himself. A titanic *blatt*, twice as loud and hot as before, scorched the seat of his favorite jeans.

Okay, he thought. *That one was me.*

"Excuse me," the girl said politely. "It seems your butt is smoking."

Darren grimaced in pain. The fart didn't just smell. It burned!

"Hang on!" The girl strolled over to the infirmary's small fridge and grabbed a handful of colored medicinal Popsicles. "Maybe these will help!"

Couldn't hurt, Darren thought. He grabbed the Popsicles, ripped off the wrappers, and jammed them down the seat of his pants. Steam rose from his backside. He was a sticky mess, but at least his butt wasn't on fire anymore.

"You're welcome," the girl said. "My name's Tina, by the way. Tina Heiney."

"Darren," he introduced himself. "And thanks."

Two more kids entered the office, clutching their stomachs.

"Say, do I detect the enticing aroma of Popsicles?" Walter Turnip asked. Darren recognized him from another fourth-grade class. As tall as he was wide, Walter was hard to miss. But today his bulging belly appeared even bigger than usual, like an overinflated balloon. He looked like a blimp in a rumpled T-shirt. And unless Darren was imagining things, Walter appeared to be floating a few inches off the floor, at least until a noisy fart released some gas and he touched down again. "Never mind. My digestive tract feels a trifle unsettled."

As always, Juan-Carlos Finkelstein was by Walter's side. He was tall, too, but in a lanky way. "I always said he was full of hot air, but this is taking it too far!"

Juan-Carlos would have been the school's number-one class clown . . . if only his jokes were funny. He was usually trying to get a laugh, but right now he seemed to have something else gurgling inside him. He made a face and scurried across the room. A moment later, an explosively loud and smelly fart went off right where he had been standing only seconds before.

Darren was impressed and disgusted at the same time. "How did you do that?"

"I don't know," Juan-Carlos said. "It's just been happening since lunch."

The nurse's office smelled like Fart Central Station. Darren figured this epidemic of flatulence couldn't be a coincidence. He looked around at the other kids.

"Did all of you eat the lunchroom burritos, too?"

"I had to," Tina said. "Somebody swiped my lunch."

"And mine as well," Walter said.

"Mine, too," said Juan-Carlos. "Or should that be 'mine, three.'"

"Make that four," Darren said. "And I'm pretty sure it was the B.O. twins." He explained that he and Andy had caught the twins lurking around the coat closet, right before his lunch disappeared. "I guess they grabbed yours, too . . . for some reason."

"Er, because they were hungry?" Tina suggested. "And too cheap to spring for their own lunches?"

"But *four* lunches?" Juan-Carlos asked. "That seems a bit extreme. One is usually enough for me."

"Speak for yourself," Walter said.

"I don't think this was just about the lunches," Darren said, remembering what he'd witnessed in the hall a few minutes before. "I think they were up to something bigger, something involving Harry Buttz. They were snooping around the basement before. . . ."

"But what does that have to do with swiping our lunches?" Tina asked.

Darren had no idea, but he had an uncomfortable feeling, and not just in his stomach.

Nurse Rancid stirred and lifted her head. "Oh my," she moaned. "What happened?"

Darren still needed a note for Miss Priscilly. He hurried toward the nurse with the notepad, but before he could even hand her the pen, a silent blast of not-so-fresh air knocked her out again. Her head drooped forward onto her chest.

Darren scowled at Tina.

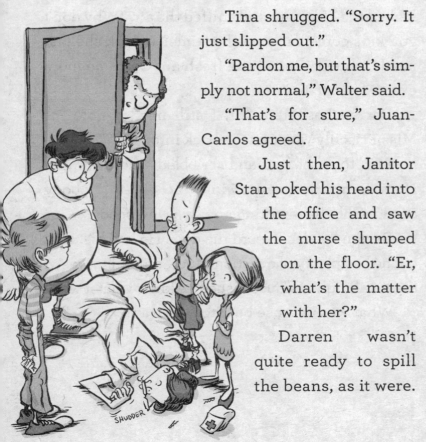

Tina shrugged. "Sorry. It just slipped out."

"Pardon me, but that's simply not normal," Walter said.

"That's for sure," Juan-Carlos agreed.

Just then, Janitor Stan poked his head into the office and saw the nurse slumped on the floor. "Er, what's the matter with her?"

Darren wasn't quite ready to spill the beans, as it were.

SHUDDER

"Beats me," he said. "Maybe she's been working too hard?"

The other kids did not contradict him. Who wanted to be known for having farts nasty enough to flatten the school nurse?

"I see," Stan said, sounding unconvinced. He looked the kids over and sniffed the air. "Why don't you kids come back another time? I think she just needs a break and a little fresh air. Or, to be more exact, *fresher* air."

Darren hesitated. "Er, I still need a note—or Miss Priscilly won't let me back into class."

Stan took the pad and scribbled a note, forging Nurse Rancid's name. He winked at Darren. "Nobody can read her handwriting anyway. Now scoot!"

Darren headed toward the door. He had his note, but he had plenty of questions, too. Something was in the air all right. He just wished he knew what it was.

What was in those burritos anyway?

CHAPTER THREE

It was recess, and the playground on the roof of the school was filled with kids enjoying the fresh air. Ordinarily Darren would be in the thick of things, trying to burn off all his excess energy, but today he kept to the sidelines, avoiding everybody but Andy. His stomach was still churning, and he was clenching hard against another gas eruption.

"Boy, those burritos really did a number on you," Andy said sympathetically. "You think you can get through class without farting again?"

"I hope so," Darren said uncertainly.

He spotted Harry Buttz and the B.O. twins hanging out together across the yard, shunned by everybody else. This was all their fault, Darren realized. If B.O. hadn't swiped his lunch, he wouldn't have had to eat those darn burritos! He wouldn't have farted in class. And he would be dreaming about sports camp instead of worrying about summer school.

His temper took over, and he stormed across the roof to confront the bullies.

"Wait!" Andy called out, but once Darren got going there was no slowing him down. "Great," Andy muttered. "Here we go again. . . ."

As Darren got closer to the threesome, he could hear Harry giving his flunkies a hard time. "You're going to have to do better next time," he scolded. "Four lost lunches wasn't nearly enough to—"

"I knew it!" Darren said, butting in, as Andy ran to keep up. Darren could only guess what Harry meant by "next time," but the part about the "lost lunches" only confirmed his suspicions.

"You people are nothing but a rotten bunch of lunch thieves!"

"Beat it, Stonkadopolis," Harry said. "Mind

your own business."

"Hey!" Bertha said, recognizing Darren and Andy. "These are the dweebs who interrupted us before."

"Yeah," Oscar confirmed. "They're the ones who spoiled things, so we couldn't—"

"Shut your trap," Harry barked, as though Oscar was about to say too much. He scowled at Darren and Andy. "Are you two deaf? Get lost."

Harry's reaction convinced Darren that the stolen lunches were part of some larger plot.

"What's this all about?" he demanded. "Does it

have something to do with you snooping around
the basement?"

"Basement?" Andy asked, completely lost.

Harry's scowl turned into a glare. "If you were
smart, you'd stop being so nosy." He nodded at B.O.
"Show these punks what happens to people who
ask too many questions."

"You bet, Number Two," Bertha said.

"Don't call me that!"

"Sorry," Oscar said on his sister's behalf.

The twins closed in on Darren and Andy
while Harry hung back, content to let B.O.
do the dirty work. Darren gulped, realizing
that he really hadn't thought this through.
He glanced around, but didn't see any
teachers watching. Not that it mat-
tered. Thanks to his family
connections, Harry got away
with a lot at Harry Buttz Elementary.

"You two got lucky before,"
Bertha said, "but not this time."

Oscar cracked his knuckles. "'Bout time you got what's coming to you."

"Hang on!" Andy took off his glasses and looked around for a safe place to put them. "I don't think I want to see this anyway."

Darren figured they were goners, unless . . .

He spun around and let loose with a volcanic fart that blasted the twins off their feet. They tumbled backward, gasping and choking at the stench. Their eyebrows were singed from the heat of the

BRRAPPATOW!!!

eruption. A few feet back, Harry's jaw dropped and his eyes widened.

"The burritos," he realized. "They must be even gassier than anyone thought possible!"

Darren grabbed Andy by the arm and dragged him away.

"Later, losers!" he said as Andy put his glasses back on. He looked around in confusion. "What happened?"

Darren just grinned.

Maybe there *were* advantages to having the hottest farts in school.

CHAPTER FOUR

Darren still needed to get back in Miss Priscilly's good graces, or kiss sports camp good-bye. "Is there any way I can earn some extra credit?" he asked.

"The town's one-hundredth birthday is coming up," the teacher said. "So why don't you write up a report on the history of Buttzville?"

Darren knew he had to get an *A* on the report. At this point, he needed all the extra credit he could get to stay out of summer school. During study hall, he and Andy headed straight for the school library. Darren was grateful for his friend's help. Andy got much better grades than Darren did, probably because he could actually sit still and study sometimes!

They took every book on the history of Buttz-ville off the shelf. Most of them were covered with dust, no doubt because no one ever read any of them. But there was one that seemed less dusty than the others: *The Buttz Family Chronicles.*

Andy cracked it open and started reading. Darren peered over his shoulder.

Herein lies a true account of the Family Buttz, the book began, *and the terrible curse that hath long afflicted them....*

"Curse?" Darren said. "That sounds interesting."

"I'll say," Andy agreed. "Listen to this...."

According to the book, the Buttzes had always been cursed with a never-ending butt itch. The curse had been passed down from generation to generation, all the way back to the old country. The Buttzes were doomed to scratch themselves forever until one of Harry's ancestors, an alchemist named Scabious Buttz, found a cure for their condition by—

The rest of the pages about the curse had been ripped out. When the book picked up again, the Buttzes were busily founding the town and making their fortune. Nothing more was written about the curse.

"What the—" Darren objected. "Where's the rest of it?"

"Gone," Andy said.

Darren was puzzled. If Scabious had found a

cure, why was Harry Buttz still scratching? Darren couldn't help wondering if this had something to do with why B.O. had stolen those sandwiches—and whatever it was Harry was up to "next time."

Darren checked to see if there was another copy of the book on the shelves, but no such luck. Frustrated, he went up to the librarian's desk. "Excuse me," he asked. "Can you tell me who checked out this book last? It appears to be damaged."

The librarian checked her records. "Harry Buttz the Second checked it out just a few weeks ago."

"Is that so?" Darren said. "I should have known."

Now Darren had to find out what was on the missing pages.

But how?

CHAPTER FIVE

The next day found Darren stuck at a school assembly and not very happy about it. He was not a big fan of school assemblies. It was too much sitting around on the bleachers in the gym, and the Harry Buttz Elementary School gym almost smelled worse than farts. It stank of chlorine so bad it made Darren's eyes water. Some genius had had the brilliant idea to build a retractable floor and put the school pool right underneath it. Assemblies were the worst. And this one was the worst of the worst—a boring presentation on the history of the town, complete with a slide show and speeches!

"Generations ago, this was just worthless

swampland," Principal Dingleberry said into a microphone down on the floor of the gym. "But from the stagnant depths of a polluted marsh rose Harry Buttz Elementary School. Mr. Buttz could not be with us today, but his illustrious family is represented by our own Harry Buttz, or, as his friends call him, 'Number Two'!"

Harry gave the principal a dirty look. She knew how much he hated to be called that. He stood beside her, squirming awkwardly, hands tucked deeply into his pants pockets.

"Bet you a week's allowance," Darren whispered to Andy,

"that Harry can't get through this assembly without scratching his butt."

"Forget it," Andy said. "I'm not dumb enough to take that bet."

Sure enough, within moments Harry was reaching around and scratching himself onstage. Snickers and giggles rippled through the audience.

"And there he goes . . . ," Andy said, grinning.

"Just like in that history book," Darren whispered, remembering what they'd read about the Buttz family curse. "I still wish I knew what those missing pages said. . . . For my report, of course."

"You know, I've been thinking about that," Andy said. "We might be able to find the answer on the Internet. If you want, we can search for it this weekend." He paused to sniff the air. "Hey, who farted?"

"Don't look at me," Darren insisted. His stomach was still rumbling like a restless volcano, but he didn't *think* that fart came from him. Glancing around, he spotted Walter Turnip sitting a few rows behind them in the bleachers. Looking rounder than ever, Walter was holding onto the bench with both hands to keep from lifting off into the air!

Uh-oh, Darren thought.

He scanned the gym until he located Tina and Juan-Carlos, who had also noticed Walter's predicament. This wasn't good. If Walter got caught floating around, the whole school—heck, maybe even the whole world—would find out just how freaky their farts had become. They exchanged looks, realizing that something had to be done. Just the fear of being exposed as an uncontrollable explosive farter agitated Darren's stomach. He guessed that the others were having the same reaction. They had to clear the gym before Walter floated away.

Darren had an idea, but it was going to take teamwork.

He took out his phone and furtively texted the others:
ON THE COUNT OF THREE...

The farty foursome nodded at one another.

"One..." Darren mouthed, raising his index finger. "Two ..." then his middle finger. "Three ..." and his ring finger....

And then they all let one rip simultaneously.

Suddenly, the entire gym reeked like the world's biggest fart. The disgusting odor was everywhere, making it impossible to tell where the fart had come from. Gagging and holding their noses, everyone dashed for the exits.

CLICKITY CLICKY CLICKITY

"This assembly is over!" the principal shouted. "Please exit in an orderly fashion!" Then she dropped her microphone and ran screaming out of the gym.

Andy was halfway to the door before he noticed that Darren wasn't following him.

"What are you waiting for?" he called. "We gotta get out of here. This place stinks, big time!"

"Don't worry about me!" Darren shouted. "I'm right behind you!"

He felt bad about lying to his best friend, but this wasn't his secret to share.

The gasping crowd carried Andy away, and

within minutes the gym was deserted except for Darren and his flatulent accomplices.

And just in time!

Superinflated, Walter lost his grip on the bleachers and shot up toward the ceiling. Random farts sent him jetting about in the air like a leaky balloon. High above the floor, he bounced off the walls and ceiling.

"Your assistance, please!" he hollered. "I can't get down!"

Darren and the others stared up at him, unsure what to do.

"Do we try to lasso him?" Juan-Carlos asked.

"I don't think I can throw that high," Darren said. "Maybe he'll run out of gas?"

Walter doubted it. "Not the way my stomach is still churning."

"Ditto," Tina confirmed.

"And all this excitement is just making it worse!"

Then, as if things weren't bad enough, Bootsie barged back into the gym, snooping as usual. "Hey! What's going on in here?"

"Er, nothing," Darren said. "Why do you ask?"

Bootsie looked around suspiciously. She hadn't spotted Walter overhead yet, but it was only a matter of time. Her nose twitched, sniffing for trouble.

"I heard somebody shouting," she insisted.

Tina came up beside her. Bootsie's nose twitched again—and she passed out on the floor.

"Bet you didn't hear that," Tina said, smirking.

"Thanks!" Darren said. He dragged Bootsie out of the way. "But we still need to get Walter down before anybody else shows up." He shouted up at the floating kid. "Try to propel yourself by pointing your butt at the ceiling!"

"But I'll crash and crack my head open," Walter yelped.

"Not if we open the pool!" Darren said. There was a full-sized swimming pool under the floor of the gym. The floors just needed to be retracted. "Juan-Carlos! Find the controls!"

"Already on it!" Juan-Carlos said. "Time for a water landing!"

A sign above the controls read DO NOT TOUCH! Juan-Carlos ignored it.

He flicked the switch. Hidden motors hummed as the gym floor split down the middle,

revealing the bright blue waters of the pool.

"C'mon, Walter!" Darren shouted. "You can do it! Just point your butt in the right direction!"

Walter rolled in the air, high above them. He tried to orient himself.

"Very well," he said nervously. "Wish me luck!"

Then a supersonic fart sent him rocketing down toward the pool.

Splashdown!

POOT

A huge wave soaked Darren, Juan-Carlos, and Tina, but they hurried to fish Walter from the pool regardless. Dripping wet, he was even heavier than he looked.

"Wow!" Juan-Carlos said. "That was a real power dive! You practically emptied the pool!"

Walter looked like he was just glad to be on solid ground again.

Darren's sneakers sloshed. The gym was flooded. They were so going to be busted.

"I'll handle this mess," Stan the janitor said. He appeared as if from nowhere, mop in hand. He winked at the kids. "You better make tracks before you end up having to answer some very awkward questions."

"Thanks, Stan," Darren said. "But—"

"Meet me by the janitor's closet," Stan said. "All of you."

Darren hesitated, wanting answers, but Tina tugged on his arm. "You heard the man. Let's go—unless you want everybody to know your butt is a biohazard!"

"Good point," Darren said, heading for the nearest exit as he wondered what in the world Stan could possibly want to talk about.

CHAPTER SIX

"I thought I smelled you coming!" Stan said.

Darren and his new friends crowded into the janitor's closet, which was stuffed with mops, brooms, and buckets.

"Sorry about the smell . . . ," Darren said. "It's like these farts are supercharged or something!"

"Is that so?" Stan seemed very interested in what Darren had to say. "Tell me more."

Darren explained how each kid's farts worked. It was such a relief to be able to talk about the farts  to *someone* outside the foursome. Walter could blast off into the air.

Juan-Carlos's farts were time bombs, going off minutes after he'd planted them.

 Tina's were stealth bombs that made no noise but stank worse than a sewer explosion. And Darren's burned like fire.

"There's nothing natural about these farts," Darren insisted.

"It's the burritos," Stan explained. "The lunch lady doesn't like to waste any food. So ever since the burritos got their bad rap and kids stopped eating them, she's taken to throwing the leftovers in the microwave every day. At this point, they've been heated and reheated so many times they're undoubtedly radioactive. I wouldn't be surprised if they glowed in the dark!"

"So mutated beans turned us into mutant beings?" Juan-Carlos joked.

"Something like that," Stan said.

"And you know this how?" Tina asked.

"Just by keeping my eyes open," the janitor said. "Trust me, I take out the trash every day, and the lunchroom has *never* tossed out any uneaten burritos."

"But nobody ever eats them," Juan-Carlos said. "Unless they have to."

"We did," Tina said. "Because the B.O. twins swiped our lunches."

"Wait a second," Darren said. "What if the B.O. twins swiped our lunches because they wanted us to eat those toxic burritos?"

"Actually, they weren't all that unappetizing," Walter said. His bulging stomach grumbled. "Is it lunchtime yet?"

"Don't even think about it," Tina said. "We're not peeling you off the ceiling again."

Juan-Carlos was still confused. "But what was the point? Why would they want to force people to eat bad burritos?"

"I'm not sure," Darren admitted. He felt like a puzzle was coming together, but he didn't have all the pieces yet. "But I'm pretty sure it was Harry Buttz's idea . . . and that he's not done yet."

Tina raised her hand. "If we don't eat the burritos again, will our farts go back to normal?"

"Possibly," Stan said, "but do you really want them to? Seems to me you've all been given some very special gifts. Smelly, but special." His voice grew more serious. "You know what they say:

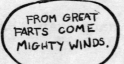

FROM GREAT FARTS COME MIGHTY WINDS.

"Er, I don't think anybody actually says that," Juan-Carlos said.

"Think about the possibilities. The question is do you want to lose your new fart abilities . . . or learn to control them?"

Darren remembered how he had bowled over the B.O. twins with a well-timed fart, saving himself and Andy from the bullies. And how he and the others had used their powers to clear the auditorium and get Walter off the ceiling. Granted, without the new fart abilities Walter wouldn't have been anywhere near the ceiling to begin with, but still, their new "gifts" had opened up a lot of possibilities for them.

"Control them?" he asked. "How?"

"I can teach you," Stan volunteered, putting on a rising-sun headband. "I can be your 'scent-sei.'"

"Good one," said Juan-Carlos. "I wish I had come up with that."

Tina raised her hand again. "Sir, why you? No offense."

"I'm the janitor," he reminded her. "Smelly stuff is my specialty."

Juan-Carlos shrugged. "Makes sense to me."

"Listen," Stan urged them, "you've already proven that you make a great team. With a little coaching, you can become . . . the Fart Squad!"

"But we're not heroes," Darren said. "Why would we need superpowers? It's not like there are any real bad guys around."

Stan shook his head in disbelief. "Are you sure about that?"

Darren thought of Harry Buttz and B.O., who he was pretty sure were up to no good. There were the stolen lunches, after all, and the way Harry and the twins had tried to sneak into the school basement afterward. They were after something, but what? Did it have to do with the Buttz family curse—and the missing pages?

"I overheard Harry say something to B.O. about 'next time,'" he told the others. "I don't know exactly what he meant, but I don't think this is over yet . . . whatever it is."

"So maybe the Fart Squad needs to be ready," Stan said.

"For what?" Tina asked.

Darren wished he knew.

CHAPTER SEVEN

"**W**elcome to Fart Boot Camp!" Stan greeted them.

The janitor used his keys to let them into the school. Darren usually hung out with Andy on Saturdays. He felt bad about ditching his friend on a weekend, especially after Andy had volunteered to help Darren with his report, but Stan had sworn the entire "Fart Squad" to secrecy. According to him, the fewer people who knew about them, the better.

Stan had set up the gym to be a secret training center, with padded wrestling mats and even a trampoline in place. A tray of freshly microwaved burritos waited on top of a wheeled cart. Stan must

have raided the lunchroom freezer. Darren tried not to think about how old the burritos might be.

"Time to power up!" Stan said. "Dig in!"

Walter, Juan-Carlos, and Tina helped themselves to the greasy "fuel," but Darren held back. He was having second thoughts about this whole Fart Squad business. True, superfarts might come in handy from time to time. But now that his flaming farts were starting to cool off a little, he was reminded of how nice it feels to have a burn-free butt.

"Who wants to go first?" Stan asked.

Juan-Carlos volunteered. "Just watch me, boys and girl. I'm cookin' with gas!"

He paused, waiting for a laugh that failed to come.

"Gas, get it?" he asked.

"I'm sure they did, Juan-Carlos. You can work on your comedy later," Stan said. "Or not," he added under his breath. Stan marked an *X* on the floor with chalk. "Why don't you plant a stink bomb here . . . and see if you can keep it from going off for a full ten seconds?"

"You bet," Juan-Carlos said, taking his place on the *X*. He concentrated hard, then hurried away before the stink bomb went off. Stan took out a stopwatch. He counted down the seconds.

"Ten, nine, eight, seven, six, five, four, three, two, one . . ."

Nothing happened. Nobody heard or smelled anything nasty.

"You laid a dud, dude," Walter teased. "To use the vernacular."

"I farted, I swear," Juan-Carlos insisted. "Cross my heart . . . and my butt!"

Stan strolled over to the *X* to investigate—just as a stink bomb went off—five seconds late. He was knocked off his feet by force of the fart.

"Whew!" he said. "That was a ripe one!"

Darren and Walter helped Stan to his feet. He wiped the tears from his eyes.

"I think you need a little more practice," the janitor said. "Timing is everything, especially where farts are concerned!"

"Tell me about it," Juan-Carlos said, blushing.

Tina raised her hand. "Let me go next, please."

Juan-Carlos stepped aside. "Go for it, Tiny."

"*Tina,*" she corrected him. "Don't call me Tiny."

"I don't know," Juan-Carlos joked. "You look pretty tiny to—"

A silent fart knocked him out. He collapsed onto a mat.

Darren stared at the petite little princess. "That was an accident, right?"

"Totally," she said sweetly. "Sorry."

They all backed away from her, just to be safe. Stan had to dump a bucket of water over Juan-Carlos's head to wake him up.

Stan eyed Tina warily. She seemed so harmless, and yet . . .

"On second thought," he said, "maybe we should

give Walter some flight practice now."

Stan fitted Walter with a crash helmet and tied a safety rope around him so they could pull him back to earth if necessary. The rest of the squad helped push the trampoline to the center of the floor.

"All right," Stan declared. "You're prepped for takeoff. Fart, fart, and away!"

Walter polished off another burrito, then let loose with a jet of gas that lifted him off the floor. For a moment, it looked like he was going to slam headfirst into the ceiling, but he changed course at the last second. He zipped around overhead like a hot-air balloon gone berserk.

"Try to control your flight," Stan coached him. "Nice smooth circles!"

But Walter was spinning and looping and

zigzagging wildly above them. He grabbed frantically for a basketball hoop to anchor himself, but
missed. Noisy farts propelled him every which way.

"Oh dear!" he shrieked. "I suspect I should not
have indulged in that second burrito!"

Darren chased after the dangling safety rope.
"Don't worry! We'll pull you down!"

He grabbed the rope, hoping to reel the flying
kid in, but Walter's farts had more lift than
he'd expected. Before he knew it,
Darren took flight as well.

"Hang on, Darren!" Tina
yelled. "Don't let go!"

She, Juan-Carlos,
and Stan pushed the
trampoline back
and forth across
the floor, try-
ing to keep it

under their airborne friends. Darren gulped when he looked down and saw how far up he was.

"Get us down!" he yelled at Walter. "This is crazy!"

"I'm endeavoring to do just that!" Walter yelled.

The extra weight began to drag Walter down. Darren pulled himself up the rope so that more of it dangled below him. Stan and the other kids grabbed the rope and pulled Darren and Walter toward the trampoline. Darren waited until it was directly beneath him, then let go of the line.

"AAAAAAA!" he screamed as he fell.

He hit the trampoline and bounced off it onto the floor. The mats cushioned his crash landing . . . a little. His poor butt was going to be black and blue, on top of being burnt.

"Don't just sit there!" Tina called. "Help us get Walter down!"

Working together, Stan and the squad finally managed to tug Walter safely down. Juan-Carlos borrowed a barbell from the gym storeroom to weigh down Walter so that he wouldn't take off again.

"Don't be discouraged," Stan told Walter. "You just need more practice."

"Wonderful," Walter said glumly. "I can scarcely wait."

Now it was Darren's turn. Stan noticed that Darren hadn't tried the burritos yet.

"What's the matter, Darren?" the janitor asked gently. "Is there a problem?"

"I'm not sure about this," Darren confessed.

"You don't realize how hot my farts get."

"I'm not surprised," Stan said. "You've always had plenty of energy to burn. But the Fart Squad needs you, Darren. You're a born leader. I can tell. Just look at how you rushed to help Walter earlier."

Darren appreciated the pep talk, but he was still uneasy. "But what if my farts are too hot to handle?"

"All the more reason to find out just how scorching they can get," Stan said. He wheeled the cart of burritos toward Darren. "These have gone cold. Let's see if you can reheat them."

"Um, we're not going to have to eat them afterward, are we?" Juan-Carlos asked. "'Cause I think I'm allergic to fart-cooked food."

"Don't worry," Stan said. "There are plenty more where these came from." He stuck a cooking thermometer into the cold burritos. "Go ahead, Darren. Bake those beans."

Darren didn't want to let the others down. He forced down half a cold burrito and turned his backside toward the rest. His stomach started gurgling right away. He felt the hot gas building inside his gut.

"Watch out!" he warned. "Fire in the hole!"

A volcanic fart erupted through the seat of his jeans. He tried to control it, but it was like a blow-torch. The thermometer blew its top. Overheated burritos exploded, spraying beans everywhere. Goopy burrito guts were splattered over every-one's hair and clothes. Even Tina was a mess.

"Noooooooooooooooooo!" she exclaimed in horror. "I've been burrito'd!"

"I'm sorry!" Darren shouted. "I told you I couldn't control it!"

Darren surveyed the damage. Thanks to him, his new friends looked like they had just gone swimming in vomit, there was a gaping hole in his pants, and he'd made a giant fool out of himself.

Not exactly the picture of a future leader.

CHAPTER EIGHT

"**S**o where were you on Saturday?" Andy asked. "I thought I was going to help you with your report?"

"Um, my folks grounded me," Darren fibbed. It was recess, and they were catching up in the school yard. Darren felt bad about lying to his friend, but what else could he do? "Thanks for offering, though."

"Get ready to thank me some more," Andy said, bubbling over with excitement. "Guess what? I found the missing pages from that old book on the Buttz family!"

Darren couldn't believe his ears. "Really?"

"Yep!" Andy couldn't wait to fill him in. "I searched around online and finally found some scans of another copy of the book." He pulled the printouts from his backpack. "It's all here—everything about the curse and the cure and what happened next."

Darren was too impatient to read through the pages. "Tell me!"

"Okay," Andy said. "As you know, legend has it

that the Buttzes' never-ending itch goes way, way back. But generations ago, Harry's great-great-not-sure-how-many-greats grandfather, Scabious Buttz, forged the Golden Scratcher, a magical golden butt scratcher that brought them some relief. The catch? There's only so much itchiness the Scratcher can handle before it gets overloaded, like a dam that's holding back too much water. At a certain point, people got worried that the Scratcher was on the verge of spilling all that concentrated itchiness all over Buttzville, so concerned citizens stole the Scratcher and buried it in a swamp where they were sure nobody would ever find it. But guess where the town eventually built the new elementary school?"

"Right on top of the Scratcher," Darren realized.

"Bingo," Andy said. "At least according to the legend, that is."

That's what Harry is looking for in the basement, Darren realized, putting more of the pieces of the puzzle together. Harry was determined to cure his itchy behind, no matter the risk to the town. But where did the bad burritos and stolen lunches fit in? Darren felt like he was still missing something.

The lunch bell rang and they headed inside, only to find a crowd of hungry kids tugging at the door to the coatroom. Miss Priscilly stood by helplessly, looking overwhelmed.

"What is it?" Darren asked, his stomach grumbling. "What's the matter?"

"Somebody superglued the lock shut," Bootsie said, eager to be the bearer of bad news. "Nobody can get to their lunch boxes!"

"That sucks," Andy said to Darren. "Looks like we're all going to have to try the lunchroom special today."

Darren's jaw dropped. "Oh my gosh," he exclaimed.

Suddenly, it all made sense, sorta. This was what Harry had wanted to do all along, to get the entire school so farty, they'd be forced to evacuate the building, so that he could get to the basement and dig up the Golden Scratcher.

"Uh-oh," Darren gasped. "This isn't good."

The very idea of Harry getting his hands on the Scratcher made Darren's stomach churn. Harry's itchy butt might be enough to push the Scratcher

over the edge and to flood the entire town with never-ending itches!

Darren thought about melting the glue with a volcanic fart, but after what happened with the beans, that didn't seem like a good idea. Even if he didn't scorch all the lunches by accident, who would want to eat food that had been farted on?

Plus, he couldn't exactly unleash a fart in front of Miss Priscilly. . . .

He had to find *another* way to stop anybody else from eating those burritos!

"I just remembered there's something I have to do," Darren told Andy. He dashed toward the cafeteria. "Gotta run!"

Darren hated ditching Andy again, but there was no time to lose. He raced into the cafeteria at top speed.

Sure enough, there were already plenty of students lined up for today's lunch: "Magic Monday Burritos." Darren shuddered at the thought of all those kids consuming the radioactive beans. The four members of the Fart Squad were one thing, but hundreds of kids farting with complete abandon would be a catastrophe. The entire school would be one big gassy chain reaction. They would have to clear out the building—and give Harry a straight shot at the Golden Scratcher.

Unless Darren did something right away.

"Excuse me!" he shouted, cutting to the head of the line. "Comin' through!"

Angry voices protested his lack of proper lunch line etiquette, but Darren ignored them. Instead he grabbed the burritos off every kid's tray, before anyone else could eat one, and started wolfing them down with his bare hands. A familiar rumble ignited in his stomach.

MUNCH
CHOMP

Time to fight fire with fire, he thought. *Just one decent fart might be enough to empty the cafeteria—and kill everybody's appetite.*

"Whoa," he warned, clutching his stomach. "Better stay away from those burritos. I feel something nasty coming on!"

The fart erupted like a volcano, charring his pants. The line behind him broke apart as gagging students scrambled to get away from the sickening odor. For a moment, Darren thought he had saved the day. Nobody else was going to be eating those burritos now!

But then a second fart erupted from him. This one was even bigger and hotter than the first. It set off the fire alarm.

And the sprinkler system.

Cold water sprayed down from the ceiling. Shrieking kids ran from the cafeteria and out of the building. A blaring siren drove everybody toward the exits. Soaked, Darren spotted Janitor Stan assisting in the evacuation, along with all the other teachers and staff.

"Oh no!" Darren realized. His plan had back-fired . . . in more ways than one.

This was exactly the kind of distraction Harry had been trying to arrange!

Darren looked around, but didn't see Harry or the B.O. twins anywhere. Buttzville was in danger, Darren realized, and it was all his fault because he hadn't been able to control the superheated gasses surging inside him. He knew he had to make things right, even if it meant gobbling more radioactive burritos. He took out his phone and texted the rest of the Fart Squad:

BASEMENT—ASAP!

Ignoring the fire alarm, he filled a tray with burritos and sprinted to the basement entrance, his sneakers sloshing noisily. Walter, Juan-Carlos, and Tina came running to join him.

"What's up?" Juan-Carlos asked. "Where's the fire?" He waited for a laugh. "Fire, get it? 'Cause, you know, the alarm?"

SQUISH SPLOOSH SQUISHY

Darren ignored him. "It's Harry Buttz!" he said. "He's after the Golden Scratcher!"

"The golden what?" Tina asked.

Darren remembered that the other Squad members hadn't heard that part of the legend yet. He quickly filled them in even as he worried about

Harry getting to the Scratcher at last. Scabious Buttz's unnatural invention had been buried for a reason. . . .

"We need to keep that Scratcher away from Harry and his goons—before they accidentally unleash an avalanche of itchiness on the whole town!"

"Hold on there!" Walter said. "An enchanted butt scratcher? Really?"

"Says the guy who can float like a balloon," Juan-Carlos pointed out.

"Touché." Walter put on his crash helmet. "So what do we do now?"

"Just what Stan trained us to do," Darren said firmly, his mind made up. "The Fart Squad needs to go into action!" He realized now that the canny janitor had been right all along. "From great farts come mighty winds!"

He held out the tray of greasy burritos.

"Eat up!"

CHAPTER NINE

The Fart Squad refueled in a hurry. Tina and Juan-Carlos scarfed down a burrito each, while Walter somehow managed to polish off two in the same amount of time. "I must say," he said with his mouth full, "I'm developing a real taste for these succulent morsels."

"Just hurry up and swallow," Darren said. "Harry and B.O. could be digging up the Scratcher at this very moment!"

Tina emitted an oddly delicate burp. "I'm ready if you are."

"Me, too," Juan-Carlos said, patting his stomach. "Let's kick some Buttz!"

They raced down the stairs, taking the steps two at a time. Darren heard banging noises and cussing down below. They rushed into the basement in time to see Harry Buttz lifting a package from a freshly dug hole in the basement floor. The B.O. twins stood nearby, sweating heavily, which made them smell even worse. Bertha gripped a shovel with both hands. Oscar held a sledgehammer. And was that a jackhammer in the corner?

"Finally!" Harry exclaimed. "I found it!" He held up a battered wooden chest about a foot long. He fumbled with a rusty latch, trying to pry it open.

"Put that back where it belongs, Harry!" Darren shouted. "It's too dangerous to mess with!"

Harry was startled by the interruption. "You again, Stonkadopolis?" He spotted the rest of the Fart Squad as well. "And you brought friends?"

"We can't let you use the Scratcher," Darren said. "It's too dangerous!"

"Try and stop me," Harry said, sneering. He nodded at B.O. "Keep them away from me, and I'll buy you all the computer games you want!"

"No problem, Number Two," Bertha said.

"Don't call me that!"

"Sorry!"

She swung the shovel at Walter, who farted in alarm. A burst of hot air shot him up to the ceiling so that the shovel passed harmlessly beneath him.

Bertha's eyes bugged out in surprise. "Huh?"

Clutching his precious package, Harry darted toward a fire exit at the rear of the basement. Darren hesitated, torn between chasing after him and staying behind to help the Squad deal with B.O.

Could the rest of the Fart Squad take care of themselves?

Tina and Juan-Carlos faced off against Bertha and Oscar, who snickered at their seemingly unimpressive opponents.

"Seriously? A little girl and a clown?" Bertha jeered. "Is this a joke?"

Tina smiled slyly. "That depends," she said politely.

"On what?" Berta said, scowling.

"On who gets the last laugh."

Tina didn't seem to do anything but just stand there primly, but a powerful odor hit Bertha without warning. The looming bully toppled backward into the hole in the floor.

"One down," Tina said.

"Sis!" Oscar cried out, suddenly finding himself

outnumbered. He raised his sledgehammer nervously. "What did you do to her?"

Tina shrugged. "Who said I did anything?"

Oscar chickened out. He bolted for the stairs. "Get out of my way, you freaks!"

Juan-Carlos darted aside to let him pass, but, just as Oscar thought the way was clear, a stink bomb went off on the stairs, knocking him backward down the steps.

He moaned at the foot of the stairs, all the fight banged out of him.

BLAP!

Darren grinned at Juan-Carlos. "Nice timing."

"I'm working on it," he said. "Now let's go get that Scratcher."

A voice from the ceiling called down to them.

"Aren't you forgetting something?" Walter said. "I wouldn't mind a little help getting down from here!"

Darren hesitated again. Harry was getting away. . . .

"Don't worry about Walter," Tina called out to Darren. "We'll help him out. You go after Harry."

"Yeah," Juan-Carlos chimed in. "Get that magic butt thingy back before we're all scratching ourselves like crazy!"

Darren trusted his squad to get Walter down from the ceiling.

Then he took off after Harry . . . and the Golden Scratcher!

CHAPTER TEN

Darren chased Harry out of the basement and up three flights of stairs. Huffing and puffing, Harry ran out onto the rooftop playground and slammed the door shut behind him. Darren grabbed the doorknob, but it refused to budge. A harsh odor seeped from the other side of the door. Darren recognized it right away.

Superglue! Couldn't Harry at least have come up with something new this time?

Harry had glued the lock shut, but that wasn't going to stop Darren. He turned around

BLATT!

and let loose with a volcanic *blatt* that melted the lock and blew down the door. Steam rose from the back of his trousers.

"Okay, that's more like it," he said, his butt still smarting from the eruption. "I had that one under control. Almost."

He rushed onto the roof just in time to see Harry pry open the lid of the wooden chest and reach inside for the Golden Scratcher. About a foot long, the gleaming instrument had curved metal claws at one end, all the better for scratching a persistent itch.

"Yes!" Harry gloated. "I can finally cure my itch!"

"Don't do it, Harry," Darren shouted. "I know about the curse, but it's too risky. You read the book. The Scratcher can't handle one more itch!"

"I don't care!" Harry snarled. "Stay out of this, Stonkadopolis. I told you before, this is

none of your business. Get lost!"

"Your buddies made it my business when they stole my lunch," Darren said.

"Those morons were supposed to take *all* the

lunches, so that everyone would eat those disgusting burritos, but then you and your nerdy buddy had to interfere so that I only got four measly lunches. *Everybody* was supposed to be farting like crazy, not just you and a few other kids. I wanted the whole school shut down!"

Darren stalled some more. "So then you tried again. . . ."

"Yes! The next time the burritos were on the menu. And now the Scratcher belongs to me!"

Darren tried to reason with Harry.

"That was buried for a reason, remember? The

Scratcher can't take any more. If it blows, you could curse the whole town with itchy butts like yours!"

"So what?" Harry said. "It would serve everybody right for laughing at me all these years." He waved the Scratcher at Darren like a weapon. "Don't even try to talk me out of this. I've been waiting for this moment for too long!"

Before Darren could stop him, Harry reached around and put the Scratcher to use. A look of supreme relief came over his face.

"Oh my goodness!" he exclaimed. "It's working! It's killing the itch!"

Darren hoped that would be the end of it, but no such luck. After a few moments, an eerie glow lit up behind Harry, and the Scratcher started humming and throwing off sparks. Visibly frightened, Harry yanked the Scratcher away from his rear. More sparks flew.

"Uh-oh," he said sheepishly.

Darren resisted the temptation to say "I told you so."

The Golden Scratcher was glowing brighter and brighter, like a nuclear power plant running out of control. Darren could tell it was too late to bury it again. The Scratcher had reached its limit and was about to burst. Generations of Buttz itches were going to spill over the entire town—unless Darren could use his farts for good!

"Throw it away!" Darren shouted at Harry. "Hurry!"

Panicked, Harry hurled the sparking Scratcher away from him. It arced through the air.

"Watch out, Number Two!" Darren shouted.

"Don't call me that!"

Using every bit of energy in his gut, Darren blasted the flying Scratcher with a fiery ball of gas that completely incinerated it. All that was left was ashes—and a charred hole at the back of Darren's pants.

"Yikes!" Harry backed away, trembling.

The rest of the squad came rushing onto the roof. Darren half expected to see Bertha and Oscar

chasing after them, but those two were nowhere in sight. "You take care of you-know-who?" he asked, pinching his nose to represent the smelly twins.

"Naturally," Juan-Carlos said. "Everyone knows that farts are stronger than B.O."

Tina looked around. "What happened to the Scratcher?"

"It's toast," Darren said. "Mission accomplished."

"Way to go, dude." Juan-Carlos high-fived him. "You're on fire. Get it?"

Tina groaned. "Yes, JC, we get it. We *always* get it."

Sirens blared below as police cars and fire engines converged on the school.

"Time to retreat!" Darren decided. He looked Walter over. "You think you can airlift all of us?"

"Absolutely." Walter fished a cold burrito from his pocket and stuffed his face. He swelled up like a hot-air balloon and started to lift off from the ground. Darren and Juan-Carlos grabbed his legs just in time. Tina scrambled onto his back and wrapped her tiny arms around his neck. "Hold on tight!" Walter said. "Prepare for takeoff!"

A tremendous fart blasted them all into the air. Walter zoomed off the roof, carrying the rest of the Squad with him. Within seconds, they were far away from Harry Buttz Elementary and the wailing fire engines. All of Buttzville stretched out below them.

"Yes!" Darren whooped. "We did it!"

Maybe this Fart Squad thing was going to be a lot of fun after all.

CHAPTER ELEVEN

Back at school, Stan took custody of the "special" burritos, saving them until the Fart Squad was needed again.

"Because that's the thing about farts," the janitor explained. "Just when you think you're all cleared out, an even bigger one comes along!"

With his farts finally under control, Darren found it easier to sit still in class. He even got a B on his report, which left out the part about the Buttz Curse and the Golden Butt Scratcher. Darren figured nobody would believe that part . . . and it would just upset Miss Priscilly's delicate sensibilities.

"A 'B' isn't bad," Andy assured him. "And every little bit of extra credit helps. You just need to find some way to burn off all that crazy energy of yours that doesn't involve getting into trouble."

"Actually," Darren said, "I think I know how to do that now."

"From great farts come mighty winds," Stan had said, and Darren believed him.

No matter the danger, the Fart Squad was ready to put the stink on the bad guys!

The End . . . for now.

Read a Sneak Peek of Book Two,
Fart Squad: Fartasaurus Rex

Out of nowhere, the tar pit bubbled and belched. It filled the air with a sour, stomach-turning smell that stank worse than a port-a-potty after a chili cook-off.

But the disgusting smell wasn't the worst thing rising from the pool of sticky black tar. Dozens of school kids on a field trip to the site stared wide-eyed at the pit. Their jaws dropped and their stomachs turned.

A gargantuan scaly head poked up from the gaseous soup. Prehistoric yellow eyes looked around at the modern world. Slimy drool dripped from hungry jaws. The tip of an enormous tail shot up from beneath the gooey surface of the pit. Bubbles burst from the tar, as if someone had let a giant fart rip in the bath, and a moment later, another nauseating burst of stink polluted the air, causing people to gag, plug their noses, and run for their lives.

FARTOSAURUS REX LIVED AGAIN!

CHAPTER ONE

EARLIER:

Darren Stonkadopolis had been looking forward to this field trip for weeks. As a die-hard dinosaur lover, Darren's favorite place to visit was the Buttzville Prehistoric Tar Pit & Museum. He never got tired of the local tourist attraction. Besides the pit itself, the museum contained fossils of ancient creatures trapped in the gooey tar millions of years ago, a museum, gift shop, and dinosaur-themed cafeteria. But the key piece of the museum's collection was the rarest of all dinosaurs, the long-extinct "Buttosaurus." It was the only one of its type and scientists believed it may have only ever existed in Buttzville.

"Check out those razor-sharp teeth," Darren said, pointing out to his best friend, Andy Blackman, as they admired the colossal skeleton, which towered above them on its hind legs outside the museum. Rows of sawlike fangs lined the dinosaur's bony jaws. "That's how you know it was a meat-eater. A predator!"

Andy probably already knew that, Darren figured. His friend was one of the brainiest kids at Buttzville Elementary School after all. But Darren couldn't resist raving about the skeleton and dinosaurs in general. They were just too cool to keep quiet about.

"Boy, wouldn't you like to see one of these in real life!"

Andy peered at the ferocious-looking skull through a thick pair of glasses. The tar had stained the bones a dark brown color. "Actually, I think I like keeping one hundred fifty million years between us."

While the entire fourth grade explored the paved pathways around the tar pit, the teacher in charge, Miss Priscilly, tried to keep all the children under control. She only had Stan, the school janitor, to help. He had also come along as an extra chaperone. The hardest kid to mind was also the richest—Harry Buttz Jr. The school and the town were named after his father. They still owned half of Buttzville. That's why Harry felt he could ignore the safety rail surrounding the pit and go in to get a closer look.

"Unhand me!" Harry squealed, when Stan grabbed him by the collar to save him from falling in. "I'll have your job!" he harrumphed as he tugged at his collar.

"Children, children!" Miss Priscilly called out. "Gather round and pay attention, while our host, Professor Paleo, kindly explains the educational value of this site."

The elderly museum curator had been conducting the tar pit tour ever since Darren was a little kid. He was a good friend of Darren's. Frizzy white hair escaped from under the pith helmet he wore. Professor Paleo winked at Darren before launching into his lecture, which Darren practically knew by heart:

"Millions of years ago, a prehistoric swamp existed where Buttzville now is. Liquid tar seeped up from the earth and created a deceptively deep pool. Dinosaurs and other primitive animals would wander over and some were unlucky enough to fall in it. Unlucky for them, but lucky for us. Their fossils were preserved in the pit when the tar hardened into thick, solid sludge. We've extracted many fossils from this site, such as that Buttosaurus skeleton on display over there. It is one of an entire genus of large-butted, vicious flesh-eating dinosaurs. Nobody knows how deep the pit goes, or what else might be trapped down there, preserved forever by the tar...."